...Until Proven Innocent
#5 in the Peter Sharp Legal Mystery Series

By Gene Grossman

From Magic Lamp Press
Venice, California

Magic Lamp Press ™

ISBN: 1-882629-51-5

The Complete
Peter Sharp Legal Mystery
Series

Single Jeopardy

…By Reason of Sanity

A Class Action

Conspiracy of Innocence

…Until Proven Innocent

The Common Law

The Reluctant Jurist

The Magician's Legacy

The Final Case

An Element of Peril

A Good Alibi

Legally Dead

Full details of these books can be seen at:
http://www.legalmystery.com

"If aliens are watching us through telescopes, they must think that dogs are the leaders of this planet. If you see two life forms, with one of them making a poop, and the other one carrying it for him, who would you assume is in charge?"

Comedian Jerry Seinfeld

1

G iven the choice, I prefer to ride in the rear seat of any nice full-sized four-door sedan. Most people don't think there's much of a difference between the front and rear seats, but in a police car, people riding in back usually don't have the option of getting out whenever they feel like it. Take it from me… I've been there.

This evening I'm riding in the front seat of an unmarked police cruiser that's being driven by 'Tony the cop,' a boat neighbor of ours who lives aboard his old wood 40-foot Newporter Pilothouse ketch. I don't know his last name or much about him, but from what I've heard, he's a not too bad of a guy, except for maybe one shortcoming: he likes to kill people.

Tony's a twenty year veteran of the police department and is now a detective sergeant. The local newspapers liken him to Clint Eastwood's *Dirty Harry* of motion picture infamy, which is probably why the police brass is urging him to 'put in his papers' and retire. Their decision is also driven by the fact that the City Council is tired of the wrongful death lawsuits he causes. His problems also extend into the local African-American community because according to some of its most vocal members, they would like to see him publicly lynched.

Aside from being a racist, fascist, bigoted killer, he seems like a pretty nice guy. A little on the silent side, but that works for me. I estimate his height to be at least six-four, because he's a couple of inches taller than me. In addition to the height, he's obviously been a bodybuilder for many years, because his bulging muscles look like they're ready to pop right through that cheap sport coat he always wears to cover up his shoulder holster. The combination of his height, muscles, sunglasses, moustache and serious grimace work very well for him on the street, and all add up to a menacing presence.

Ordinarily I wouldn't be associating with a person of his reputation, but today I don't have a choice because the senior managing partner in our law firm promised that I'd be his guest for a Mexican dinner while he explains some problem he's having with ex-wife about the child support he's paying her.

I always seem to be getting involved in strange cases at the request of my boss, but she helps out quite a bit. Being a computer whiz, she occasionally acts in an unofficial capacity to help the local police out with some hi-tech snooping. In return, they provide her with helpful information on some our criminal cases. From what I understand, we owe Tony a favor or two for some things he did for us on a past case, so that's why I'm now on the way to his favorite Mexican dive in Culver City, where he'll probably pour his heart out to me about the mean ex-wife. So far he hasn't said anything, but that'll probably change once we get to the restaurant.

It's seven on a Wednesday evening and the place is almost empty. There's a long bar on the left side of the room, some tables in the middle, and six booths along the right side. Tony heads for the last booth and sits down with his back to the wall, so he can see the whole place. That's a paranoid habit most cops develop. I sit down opposite him, but can still see most of the place in the mirrored wall behind Tony.

The waitress finally breaks away from the two or three bar patrons and slinks over to our table.

"Hi, Tony. I had the cook start a Mexican Pizza when I saw you pull into the parking lot. It'll be ready any time now." She places two cold bottles of beer on the table. I can tell this is a real neighborhood joint because she doesn't bring any glasses.

We pick up our respective bottles, clink them together as a macho toast, and take a refreshing swig while the waitress sets our smoking hot appetizer down on the table between us. Unlike the pizzas prepared at Shakey's, this one is a large flat plate of beans and rice heaped on top of large chips, all smothered in melted cheeses. I don't know what the cholesterol and fat count of this deadly dish is, but I think Doctor Kevorkian could successfully use it on some of his patients.

Waiting for Tony to speak to me, I break off a mouthful-sized chunk of this suicide platter. While looking toward the bar, Tony seems to be reaching down to scratch his leg. Just as I put the chunk into my mouth, he decides to finally speak. It's almost a whisper.

"When I say 'now,' I want you dive down in the booth. It might even be better if you made it all the way under the table."

This is a first. I've been out to dinner with a lot of people, but no one has ever said that to me. I then realize that he wasn't reaching down to scratch his leg. He was removing a snub-nosed revolver from an ankle holster. I can see in the mirror that there's a black man standing near the bar and cautiously looking around the room.

Suddenly it happens. The standing black man reaches under his jacket and removes not one, but two large handguns that were tucked into his belt. He points one towards the bar and the other towards our booth and shouts out.

"Nobody move. Anybody move, and they're dead!"

I'm now sitting here nervously trying to make a decision. Should I dive under the table immediately, or wait for Tony's command?

Unfortunately the decision is made for me, because when the bartender notices that the robber is glancing over in our direction, he pulls out his own gun and takes a shot at the black man. At that instant, three things happen simultaneously. The robber fires back at the bartender, Tony shouts 'now' at me, fires two quick shots at the robber, and I sit here frozen in place, watching the whole show in the mirror. After firing at the robber and hitting him, Tony jumps out of the booth, runs over to the guy lying on the ground and kicks the guns out of his reach. I don't think the dead criminal was in any condition to reach for them, but I guess that's what cops are trained to do.

When Tony returns to the booth, he seems upset.

"I thought I told you to get down in the booth. You didn't move. You just sat there."

"Well yeah, I didn't want to miss the show."

I hear some sirens in the distance, so the cavalry must be on the way. Tony must think I'm either completely crazy, or the coolest character on the planet. He calms down a bit and lets me know that I'm on my own for a ride home.

"You might as well finish the pizza… it'll be on the house. When the uniforms get here, I'll be busy for the rest of the night. That's the big problem with shootings – there's too much paperwork involved. You better plan on taking a cab back to the Marina."

When the men in blue come in through the front door, Tony stands up and displays his badge. They take his weapon and escort him outside. For some strange reason, the whole incident has made me hungry, so I'm now pigging out on the pizza while waiting for them to come and take my statement. I'm sure that the police brass and the City Council will be unhappy with tonight's event. Too bad they won't even take into consideration the fact that Tony stopped an armed robbery and probably saved the lives of several people, one of them being especially important to me.

2

Last night's Mexican restaurant incident is leading all the local morning news shows. It took about an hour for me to explain what happened to the three different detectives who interviewed me and kept asking the same questions over and over again. Tony called this morning and apologized, explaining that they make an extra effort interviewing witnesses whenever a police shooting is involved. When leaving the restaurant last night to get into the cab, I noticed that there were several news helicopters circling. Their videotaped views of the neighborhood, complete with flashing squad car lights and an ambulance, are now on the screen while the newsreader explains about how our city's 'Dirty Tony' has struck once again. It seems like they can't make their mind up about him. They're torn between portraying him as a hero or a trigger-happy lunatic.

While sitting here watching the news and eating a large bowl of cold breakfast cereal, I look over to the couch and see that I now have an audience. A kid and a dog.

The kid is Suzi, our law firm's senior managing partner, who's an adorable pre-teen Chinese girl with a genius IQ. The dog is her huge Saint Bernard, who I call 'Bernie.' Suzi was the stepdaughter of Melvin Braunstien, an old law school classmate of mine and former employer. When he died in a plane crash, his instructions stated that I was to be appointed as her legal guardian. When I took his place as the firm's licensed adult and was brought in as a junior partner I discovered that Suzi had always been the real brains behind Melvin's firm. With the help of some successful legal victories and several large fees, we were able to trade up from Melvin's houseboat to another client's 42-foot Californian, and ultimately to my dreamboat, the one we're living on now - a gorgeous 50-foot Grand Banks trawler yacht.

At first glance most people think that I'm an experienced boater, but Suzi knows the truth... I don't even know how to start the engines.

My audience is obviously waiting for me to make a full report on the shooting last night, so I don't disappoint them. As usual, I'm the only one who talks. After a half hour description that covers everything including the ride to the restaurant, the greasy food, the beer without the glass, the shooting, the police interviews and the taxi ride back, they both get up and exit to the little princess' domain, her private stateroom in the bow of the boat. Before they leave, the dog makes one last inspection tour to search for cereal droppings.

I guess that Tony's recent marksmanship display shoves his domestic situation to the back burner, but I'm sure I'll hear about it soon enough, because once again he's been placed on administrative leave. That's what the city calls it, but if you're told to go home and still get paid, I call it a vacation.

I can't help but notice a steady stream of people going to his boat each day, including police public relations, police union delegates, police brass, news people, and some other sorts that I can't classify by just looking at them.

There are some large soft paws pitter-pattering into my stateroom. The only thing that makes a sound like that on this boat is the dog, bringing me a message. For some strange reason, the kid rarely talks to me. Communications on our boat are usually sent by dogmail, which consists of a message tucked into Bernie's collar.

This is a very economic way of sending mail. The only cost involved is the messenger's tip, which consists of a pat on the head and a "good boy" compliment. This message tells me that tomorrow I'm to accompany Tony the 'offbeat' cop to a police shrink's office. This isn't something I'm looking forward to. Over the past several years I've become acquainted with quite a few police officers, and they all have the same mindset in common. Once they've been sworn in and get to wear the badge and gun, there are only two types of people in the world – cops and bad guys. They know that they can depend on any other cop in the country to watch their back, and the rest of the people out there are nothing more than possible future suspects in all the bad things that are sure to happen.

The unfortunate part about their philosophy is that it keeps them from becoming friendly with that large part of the population not wearing badges. I guess it's because they don't want to get close to people who they might have to arrest someday. They want to keep their distance because it helps them to believe that even the most innocent-looking citizen is guilty of a crime.

Personal feelings aside, I'll do this for the kid. I have no idea why she wants me to go with him, but I've learned not to question her messages. She always has some reason that's better than any objection I can ever come up with, so I just do as I'm told.

Whenever there's a police-involved shooting, the assumption is that it's a traumatic experience for the cop who did the shooting, so they routinely require a visit to the shrink, who must make an official recommendation that the officer is emotionally and psychologically fit to return to regular active duty.

To avoid the possibility of familiarity, they use a rotating system so that no officer ever knows what psychologist he'll be visiting until the actual time of the appointment. Tony is scheduled for a one o'clock session tomorrow afternoon at the shrink building on Hollywood Boulevard, just a few blocks west of Vine Street.

The other part of the message is a reminder to return Olive's telephone call. She's already called three times and I'm told that she's starting to sound desperate.

Stuart Schwarzman is a close friend of mine, and one of the most entrepreneurial people I've ever met. In the last year alone, he's been extremely successful in starting businesses that provide a variety of products and services, including weight-loss juice, used Toyota Camry's that he has trucked out from New Jersey, an armored car business called "he's taking it with him" that's hired by disgruntled heirs for funeral processions, and most recently, a service that imports young Thai girls for prospective

American husbands. These activities are all in addition to his growing private investigation service that has proven itself very helpful in some of our firm's recent lawsuits.

Stuart is usually good for about one fantastic new idea every six months, and he tries to get me involved in each one. Up to now I've avoided the temptation but he still keeps trying. He's due for a new one any time now.

Stuart's right-hand man is a former porno producer named Vinnie Norman, who along with his fiancée Olive, both drive armored cars for Stuart and take part in the private investigations. I tuck the note in my pocket and make a mental note to return her calls at my next opportunity. I would do it now, but the dog is sitting in front of me holding a leash in his mouth. This can only mean that he wants to take me out for my walk. He enjoys going with me because it means he gets a chance to ride in my big yellow Hummer, where he can stick his head out of the open sunroof and pretend like he's flying. And he really does look like he's flying, because before he can get his face into the wind, I have my instructions to attach his 'Doggles,' which are aviator-styled eye-protection goggles designed especially for dogs who want to stick their heads out of moving cars. Bernie sits in the front seat with his head sticking up out of the car's open sunroof. With his aviator goggles on and large ears flopping in the wind, we're a popular subject for tourists' cameras as we motor down the street.

The reason we go in the car is because I refuse to pick up after him. Our neighborhood has a pooper-scooper law that says nobody should walk a dog on the public streets without having some scooping device to use. I have nothing against following the law, but there are some things that I just refuse to do, so we go to a dog park where he can run around and do things that I don't know about, somewhere where I can't see him.

Now that the dog has taken care of his business, it's time for me to take care of mine, so I call Stuart's Van Nuys warehouse. Olive answers the phone. She recognizes my phone number on her caller ID display.

"Oh, Mister Sharp, I'm so glad you called."

Her voice becomes hushed, as if she's whispering into the phone.

"Please, can I come and talk to you?"

"Olive, if this is about that prenuptial agreement you and Vinnie were talking about, I've already told you that I won't advise either one of you about it."

"No, no, this has nothing to do with that. It's something else completely. I have a problem. Someone is threatening me."

"Olive, are you in physical danger, because if you are, I can be there in less than thirty minutes. What about Stuart and Vinnie, are they around anywhere?"

"No, it's not anything physical. Listen, Vinnie and Stuart will be back from lunch any minute now, and I don't want them to know anything about this. Can I come to the boat? Please?"

I've known Olive for almost a year now, and to the best of my knowledge, the only thing that freaks her out is dead bodies, so I'm really curious to find out what's bothering her now.

Stuart and his group have been to the boat many times, so Olive is quite familiar with these surroundings and makes herself comfortable on the couch in the boat's main saloon. I used to call that area of the boat the 'salon,' but was corrected by several of our dock neighbors, who told me that if I want to fit in around here, I'll have to call what the old sailors did: the 'saloon.' As I walk over to greet her, I notice that the forward stateroom door is slightly ajar, and just below the doorknob level I see an eye peering out. The kid never misses out on anything.

Olive starts right out by swearing me to secrecy. I explain to her that anything she tells me is protected by lawyer-client privilege, even if it involves a matter that I decide not to represent her on. Once she feels confident that Vinnie won't find out what she tells me, she starts her explanation.

"I'm being blackmailed."

"C'mon Olive, you're not a rich person. What could a blackmailer possibly expect to get out of you?"

"He wants me to sleep with him."

"Okay Olive, suppose you start out right at the beginning, because it sounds like I have some catching up to do with the facts of this alleged blackmail. First of all, exactly what is it that this person has on you?"

"You're sure that no one will know about this?"

I nod affirmatively until she once again feels at ease.

"Okay here it is, Mister Sharp, and I hope you won't think poorly of me for this, but a couple of years ago I was really having a tough time finding a job, so I answered an ad in some Hollywood magazine. They were looking for girls to work the telephones. At first I thought it would be like selling magazines or something like that, but when they told us that we could earn up to twenty dollars an hour with no selling involved, I got a little nervous. The guy went on to explain to us how lonely men wanted to talk to girls on the phone, and that they'd pay by the minute if someone would excite them."

"Olive, if I understand you correctly, you're describing what they call 'phone sex.' Is that right?"

"Well yeah, I guess you could call it that, but we never met anyone face to face, and there was definitely no touching or anything like that involved. All I did was follow the scripts they gave us, and talked to those lonely men on the phone. I had a trainer who taught me some of the special things to say. Things that the callers usually wanted to hear."

"I'm not here to judge you, Olive. You did what you had to do to make a living. That's okay with me. Now what about this threat you mentioned?"

"Oh yeah, that. Well anyway, I guess that someone in the business office of that company was bribed or something, because one of the guys who was a steady customer got hold of my home phone number. He was a repeat caller, and always asked for me by my phone name of Bambi. He started calling me last week and he knows my real name. He says that if I don't meet with him, he'll tell my boyfriend what I used to do for a living."

This sounds like a story right out of one of O'Henry's short stories written by William Sydney Porter. Olive, the former phone-sex operator is embarrassed to have her boyfriend Vinnie, the former porno director, find out about her past occupation.

Wait a minute. If she's so worried about Vinnie finding out, then she must not know about his past in the porno business. I better tread very carefully here.

"Olive, what did Vinnie do for a living before you met him?"

"Before he started working with Stuart, he told me he was with a major motion picture studio for several years, working in some department like props or wardrobe."

No wonder she's worried. Vinnie never told her about his past, so she thinks he's as white as the driven snow. This is an awkward situation because the only way to really make her comfortable in confessing her past to Vinnie is to let her know about his shady past.

That's a decision I can't make. If Vinnie wants her to know how many porno films he produced and directed, he'll have to tell her himself. It's not my job to 'out' him. The last time I looked at my business card, it said 'Peter Sharp, attorney at law,' and not 'Peter Sharp, gossip monger.'

Now that I see the direct and truthful approach isn't available to us, we'll have to deal with this blackballing sleazeball in a different, more creative way.

"How does he want you to reach him? Did he give you his name or phone number?"

"All he gave me was his cell phone number, and told me to call him Hal."

I take the cell phone number from Olive and tell her that I'll take care of everything.

3

Once again I'm in the front seat of Tony's unmarked squad car, hoping that our ride today doesn't end up as exciting as the last one.

"Tony, are you wearing that ankle holster again?"

"Yeah, but don't worry. I guarantee you that I won't be using it today."

"Really? That sounds encouraging. What did you do, swear off shooting people?"

Hearing this question brings the faint trace of a smile to his face. He reaches under his sport coat.

"Naw, if any trouble comes up, I'll be using this."

Tony brings his hand out from under the sport coat and I see that he's holding what looks like a small hunting rifle. Not being satisfied just showing it to me, he decides to give me the full fifty-cent tour.

"Mister Lawyer, this is a Smith & Wesson Model 500, and it makes Clint Eastwood's .44 Magnum look like a peashooter. This weapon's muzzle energy is more than 5 times what his was. Its overall length is fifteen inches, weighs in at over six pounds, has an eight-inch barrel, carries five rounds, and is the most powerful legal production revolver in the world. You oughta come out shooting with me some afternoon. At least once a week I go to a target range in Agoura Hills. If you want, I'll let you fire off a couple of rounds. This new model retails for over nine hundred dollars, but I can get you a deal on one if you're interested."

"Tony, I really appreciate the offer but I used up my fascination with firearms in the army, and they frown on lawyers bringing cannons into court nowadays, so I'll have to give it a pass."

I don't know why anyone would want to carry a powerful weapon like this, but in view of the fact that there are bad guys out there with AK-47 assault rifles, I guess it doesn't hurt to avoid being outgunned. From the .50 caliber designation, I guess every shot is as powerful as one coming from a .50 caliber machine gun, like the ones they put on fighter planes. Tony tells me that Smith and Wesson was planning on also bringing out a larger .64 caliber model, but they've had some opposition from the United States Government, who in what Tony claims is their ultimate stupidity, consider anything larger than .50 calibers to be 'artillery,' and therefore not desirable for civilians to own.

It's amazing to me that they'll allow these .50 caliber revolvers to be bought by the general population, considering the fact that there's some fear that the regulation police bullet-proof vests might not stop a .50 caliber round fired from one of these small cannons.

Tony also apologizes for inviting me to that gunfight the other night. He recognized that robber when the guy walked into the restaurant, having seen his picture on a list of recent releases from the penitentiary, all of which were reporting to parole officers in our jurisdiction. We'll never know how many people might have gotten killed that night If Tony hadn't acted the way he did, because I'm sure that guy wouldn't want to leave any witnesses... and one successful robbery certainly might lead to many more.

They can say all they want about this lunatic cop, but if it wasn't for him, I might not be alive today. The interesting thing about the whole affair is that it looks like it didn't shake Tony up in the least.

I graciously accept his apology and we ride the rest of the way to Hollywood in silence. He might be crazy, and I don't particularly like him very much, but I feel very safe when he's around.

The shrinks are all in an old thirteen-story building on Hollywood Boulevard just east of Highland Avenue. You can tell the building is old because there's an elevator operator mechanically working an ancient hand lever, or an ancient elevator operator working a mechanical lever... either description would be correct. He's wearing one of those bellboy uniforms, complete with the little cap. As we enter the elevator we're greeted with a "floor please?"

We get off on the eleventh floor and walk down a long marbled hallway to the end, where the 'Psychiatric Evaluations, Inc.' sign is engraved on a doorplate. Tony stops me before we go in.

"I just want you to know that the main reason I want you here is to keep this shrink honest. If I tell him that my lawyer is with me, maybe he'll give me a fair shake."

"What are you worried about? I was there. Everyone in that bar will testify that you did the right thing."

"Yeah, but that's not what this is all about today. Here, they want to see how bad you feel and how shook up you are. And I'm not. That's the problem. If I don't act like I'm at least shook up a little, they might think I'm nuts. They started wanting to get me off the force several shootings ago, and I don't want to give them any openings here today."

Nice. He's a serial killer, too. I assure him that the shrink is a professional, and that if he tells the guy about his past experiences in combat as a U.S. Marine, and about all the gunfights he's been in as a cop, that the shrink will realize he's dealing with a true professional who can keep his head together during and after a deadly situation. This is such a good line that even I believe it.

He feels a little better hearing that, so we go inside the office and are greeted by a woman who's on the verge of hysteria. This is not a good sign for a shrink's office. She immediately notices which one of us looks more official, runs over to Tony and grabs his arms.

"Are you the police? Please tell me you're the police."

"Yeah, I'm the police. I'm supposed to see a…"

Hearing that he's a cop, she cuts him off mid-sentence.

"Thank God you're here… he's still out on the ledge. I think he's really going to jump this time."

I've got to hand it to Tony. He stays as cool as a cucumber. "Has he done this before?"

"Yes. Last month he did the same thing, but we talked him back in off the ledge. I'm afraid he's really going to jump this time."

23

"Yeah I know, you already told me that. Is there a window that opens anywhere near where he is on that ledge?"

She nervously points to one of the office's other windows. It's next to the only one that has been opened.

"What's this guy's first name?"

"It's Christopher."

Tony walks over, opens the window, sticks his head out, looks both ways, and then spots the jumper.

"Hey Chris, I've got a couple of questions to ask you."

I can't see the jumper, but we're far enough up off of the street so that the noise of the traffic doesn't drown out his voice.

"Don't try to stop me. I'm going to jump today."

"Yeah, I know you're gonna jump. I'm not here to stop you, I just wanna know if your car is in the garage, because if we don't get it outa here tonight, the office will have a ton of paperwork to fill out."

"You mean you're not one of those crisis negotiators? They didn't even send a crisis negotiator? They sent one last time."

"Yeah, but that was last month, before the budget cuts. We don't send crisis negotiators anymore. They sent me to get your information, because once you hit the ground, there's really not much to scrape up. Anyway, is your car in the garage? And if it is, do you know what level it's on?"

"You know, you're crazy. I'm out here on a ledge, and you're asking me questions about my car."

"Chris, I agree that one of us is crazy, but let's face it. You're the one out there on the ledge. Now are you gonna tell me about your car, or should I just shoot you?"

Tony draws his stainless steel cannon out of its shoulder holster and waves it towards the jumper. I hear fear in the guy's voice.

"What are you going to do, shoot me with that thing?"

"What the hell do you care? You're gonna jump anyway. Our new policy is that once you've tried a stunt like this, the next time, we make sure you go through with it. Do you have any idea how much it costs the City to send those fire engines and police over here every time you pull a stunt like this? If we don't put a stop to it, you'll just keep doing it, and then we'll be so short of funds, we'll have to lay off some cops.

"Now you've got two choices, either jump, or go back through your window and sign the papers I've brought with me, promising not to do this anymore. We're getting sick and tired of jerks like you wasting our time and money."

Tony has now holstered his cannon and is waving a legal-looking document at the guy. I'm completely flabbergasted. Now I'm convinced. Tony is as crazy as the guy out on the ledge. To my surprise, Tony withdraws his head from the open window, and closes it.

"What happened, Tony? Did he jump?"

"Naw, he went back into his office. Excuse me, I'm supposed to check in with the receptionist about my appointment."

25

That was it. Tony didn't give it a second thought. The receptionist was still shaking, but Tony calms her down, hands her his card, and says that he's here to see one of the doctors. She's obviously still in a state of shock, but out of pure force of habit tells him to go down the office hallway to room 'B.' Tony motions for me to come with him. This is really strange. He'll kill a robber and threaten a jumper, but it looks like he's afraid to go into a shrink's office without me at his side. I might as well go along and watch the rest of this show, so I follow him down the hall.

Seated behind the desk is a neatly dressed gentleman in his late fifties. He seems very calm, picks up a folder with Tony's name on it, and starts his usual psychobabble.

"Hmmm. Let's see, what do we have here? Ah, I see. A police officer that seems to take delight in shooting black people, and shows no remorse about it."

I can see that this guy's trying to build up his fee. He'll probably suggest that Tony's not ready to return to active duty, but after a couple of months of treatment, maybe he'll be cured. I look at the nameplate on his desk. The first name after 'Dr.' is 'Christopher.' I look at Tony with a question on my face, and he responds with a slight affirmative nod, letting me know that we're now in the presence of the ledge guy.

Doctor jumper continues. "Detective, have you brought with you the certification sheet for your return to active duty?" I think I'd better hold on to it for a while, because we should meet a few more times."

That's it. I've heard enough. Not only is this shrink certifiable, he's a crook too. I grab the document out of Tony's hand, stand up, lean over the desk, and give Chris some advice.

"Listen here, you nutcase. Lucky for you the jump attempt ended before the news helicopters arrived, so no one really got a good enough look at you. You were standing on a ledge that was near the corner of the building above a protruding sign for the savings and loan downstairs, so they couldn't see your face from the street either. Now here's the deal. You sign this document, Detective Tony goes back to work, you don't screw the City out of any money, and we all tell the papers that it must have been one of your patients out there. We don't know who your patients are, and you don't have to tell them who it was, because of doctor-patient privilege.

"That leaves everyone happy, Tony's working again, and your alleged career as a shrink is still intact. The alternative is that you get arrested right now for perpetrating a fraud on the City, and you spend the rest of your life in a loony bin. So what's it gonna be, doc?"

The shrink looks up at me with an icy stare, removes a pen from the gold matching set on his desk, signs Tony's certificate, and we both walk out of his office.

There's not much conversation in the car on the way back to the Marina, other than my asking Tony one question. "How did you know he wasn't going to jump?"

"Elementary, counselor. His shoes looked like they'd just been worked on by that shoeshine guy in the lobby, because I could see ink polish stains on the ledge. Nobody who intends to jump off an eleventh story ledge has his shoes shined first. Besides, unless the guy's a complete psycho, he's probably a coward. He's afraid to face the problems that he's got, like a cheating wife, too many bills, stuff like that. They think that being out on a ledge will get them some attention. When he saw me waving this big pistola in his direction, he got to see what death really looks like, and that scared the hell out of him. How about you? How did you know about that protruding sign under the ledge?"

"I lied."

Tony actually cracks a slight smile at hearing my answer. "Well, it worked. That guy was really going to work me over if you weren't there. If I didn't get certified quick, I'd be in line for some prosecution for that off-duty shooting, because I didn't identify myself first by shouting out "police!" Those are the rules, you know. Next they'll probably require us to wear tee-shirts with big bulls eyes painted on, so the bad guys can have an easier target to hit. And from what I hear, that broad who's the new district attorney is a real ball-buster. You're a criminal lawyer, do you know her?"

"Yeah, you could say that."

I can tell that the computer in his brain is spinning. After a few minutes, he looks at me and says. "Oh yeah, you're the one. Now I remember. Well, I owe you."

"It's funny you should mention that. I've got a little situation I need some help with. Some sleazeball is harassing my friend's fiancée."

"You want me to talk to him?"

28

"I don't want him killed. I just want to know who he is. I can handle it from there."

I give him the note that Olive gave me.

"Here's his cell phone number."

Tony doesn't say anything. He takes the note and sticks it in his pocket. It's a nice quiet conversation-less ride back to the Marina.

4

Back at the boat, I'm greeted with a dogmail message that urges me to call a Miss April May. This name sounds like a joke of some sort, but the kid usually screens the calls pretty good, so it's probably real. I dial her number and the sweetest, sexiest, most sensual feminine voice I've ever heard answers the phone. I immediately conjure up a picture of some gorgeous female to match the voice, sit back on the couch, and in my sick mind get ready to enjoy a conversation with some sexy supermodel.

After a brief exchange of small talk, she explains that she's being evicted from her apartment because of her tiny Chihuahua.

"April, is there anything in your lease that prevents you from having a dog live with you in the apartment?"

"No, it's not that he's living with me, it's what he does outside."

"Okay, I give up. Exactly what does he do outside that is causing your eviction?"

"He does his business."

Other than the huge beast that lives with us on the boat, I don't know much about dogs, but if by 'doing his business,' she means that he leaves a souvenir on the ground, I can't imagine Chihuahua droppings as a reason for eviction.

"Why is that causing you to be evicted, April?"

"Well, that's not exactly what's causing me to be evicted, but the manager of the apartment building told me that if I didn't move out, he'd turn me in to the police for multiple violations of the dog dropping laws, and that I'd lose Charlie and probably go to jail."

Having the brain of a brilliant lawyer, I put two and two together and figure that Charlie must be the little rat she calls a dog.

"April, if the law he's talking about requires you to pick up your dog's droppings, have you been doing that?"

"No Mister Sharp, I haven't. I've got a slight problem with my back, and it's too hard for me to bend over to pick Charlie's stuff up. Mister Sharp, I'm really worried about this. And I'm not the only one he's been threatening. There's a nice older couple living upstairs of me, and he says that they're moving out too. I don't see them very often."

"April, just how old is that 'older' couple?"

"Oh my goodness, they must be almost fifty."

At this point my image of a life with April has just disappeared. She's obviously a twenty-something bimbo who thinks that everyone over thirty is a senior citizen. Besides, if I were ever to go out with a supermodel, I'd have the fear that if we were involved in an auto accident she'd place a higher priority on her broken nail than on my broken leg.

I tell April that she should call Suzi to make an appointment to come and see us. She tells me that Suzi already told her to come by this afternoon, so she'll be at the boat in an hour. This gives me some time to try and find out why our law practice has

31

sunk lower than merely 'going to the dogs,' we're now down to the dog droppings.

The answer to today's mystery is solved when the phone rings and my caller display shows Olive's cell phone number.

"Hello Olive. Before you ask, I just want you to know that I'm already working on that guy who's bothering you. We should have some information on him later this week."

"Oh thanks, Mister Sharp, but I was only calling to see if you had a chance to speak to April."

"She's a friend of yours?"

"Well, sort of. I was with Suzi a couple of times when she took Bernie to the dog park, and he's really friends with Charlie... that's April's dog."

"Yeah, I know. You mean that the huge Saint Bernard and the tiny Chihuahua are friends, and they play together?"

"Oh, yes. They're great friends. And you know what? After hearing April, I recognized her as being my trainer at the Love Line, that place where I worked doing that phone stuff. She was the one who broke me in, and I tried to sound just like her when talking to the customers. She taught me how to find out the special things that each caller wanted to hear, so that when they called back again, I could pretend like they were special and that I remembered them."

That answers another question. I'm glad to see that a sweet sexy voice like April's was put to some good use. My curiosity gets the best of me and I don't want to wait to find out.

"Olive, would you please tell me what April looks like?"

There's a slight hesitation on the other end of the phone. I don't know if Olive's still there, or if her cell phone dropped the call.

"Olive? You still there?"

"Yes, I'm still here. You wanted to know what April looks like. Well, let's say she's put on a few pounds recently, and it hasn't exactly helped her appearance any."

Okay. In a way I'm glad she's on the chubby side. This will keep me from falling for her when she talks to me.

A large boat must be moving somewhere close to ours, because the Grand Banks is starting to rock in the slip. There's a megayacht parked at the end of our dock that I've been told belongs to George Clooney. Thinking that the rocking is being caused by George's boat pulling out, I walk over to the window to see if he's up on the bridge. George's boat is still there and I now see what's causing our boat to rock. April is coming up the boarding steps. She walks into the saloon and fills up the room. I don't think I've ever met anyone this fat. She must weigh close to five hundred pounds. Charlie is with her, but he immediately runs to the forward stateroom to visit with his friend Bernie, who signaled his presence with a soft whine. I tell April to sit down and relax and offer her a cold glass of water. She broke a sweat coming up our boarding steps. Later on I'll check to see if she broke the steps too.

I'll never know how people can possibly let themselves go like this. She probably has no control over her poor complexion, but boy, that body sure needs work. She obviously knows what's going through my mind, because it's the same thing that everyone thinks when seeing her for the first time.

"I guess now you can see why I have difficulty picking up Charlie's droppings."

"Well April, I don't have to tell you that it would help if you lost a few pounds, but in the meantime, there are those small dustbins on a pole, like the kind that ushers use in a movie theater to pick up cigarette butts. If you really want one, I'm sure that every pet store has them for sale. Then you won't have to bend down at all."

"I know, Mister Sharp, but I don't think it would help now. The manager told me he's already got another tenant lined up for my apartment, and also one for the place upstairs where those older folks live.

"You know, the strange thing is, we're not the only ones in the building with dogs. There're lots of them. But we're the only ones he's picking on."

This sounds like a coincidence, and I don't like coincidences. I tell April to write down all the information about her building, how long she's been there, and any information she has on Mister Miller, the manager.

"April, you can stay here as long as you want this afternoon, because I know that Charlie and Bernie need some time together. I've got some errands to run, so if you'll excuse me, I'll be taking off now."

"Thank you for helping me, Mister Sharp. About your fee…"

"Oh, you can make those arrangements with Suzi. She usually handles things like that."

"Yes, I know. I've already talked to her about it, and we agreed that you would let my boyfriend arrange to take care of it."

Wow. She's got a boyfriend. I don't even want to know what he looks like. Well, that's another problem I don't have to worry about. I can always have Tony the cop talk to April's building manager, and I'm sure that once he sees that .50 caliber cannon of Tony's, he'll change his mind and let April stay there. If Suzi gets more than a hundred bucks out of April's boyfriend, I'll be happy.

I don't really have any errands to run this afternoon, but I don't want to sit and chat with April for another hour or so, and it looks like that's how long it would take for her to get up enough strength to leave the boat. While I've got some time, I might as well take a ride over to her apartment building and see what it looks like.

Most of the buildings in Santa Monica are kept up very nicely, and her two-story apartment building is no exception. It's less than two blocks away from the ocean, but there's nothing that blocks most of the building's view, because the only things between her building and the water are a McDonald's Restaurant and a couple of large parking lots for some office buildings. The first two levels are for parking, so April lives on what is equivalent to the third floor above the street level.

I follow a delivery person who gets buzzed through the locked front doors, and by walking through the hallways I locate April's apartment number.

Back outside the building, I look up and discover the particular apartments that April and her upstairs senior citizen neighbors occupy are the only two bedroom corner units with a clear ocean view. The other side of the building has two more units like that, but their ocean view is partially obstructed by some new skyscraper that's being constructed.

This time, I do it the proper way. I ring the manager's bell and wait to be buzzed through the doors. He comes out and meets me in the elevator foyer. I don't like him at first sight. He's a swarthy guy with a thin moustache and long black oily hair swept back into a ponytail, all covered by a dark porkpie slim-brimmed hat, and he's wearing a pair of dark sunglasses. If I didn't know better, I might think that he's a member of some bebop jazz combo that plays in hip San Francisco basement clubs. His small goatee makes him look like a combination computer image of Dizzy Gillespie, Miles Davis, and Chet Baker. He doesn't give his name or offer his hand. There's a terse greeting.

"I'm the manager here. What do you want?"

What a charmer this guy is. Now that all forms of professional courtesy have been eliminated, I get right to business.

"I'm moving out here from Chicago in a month or two for an assignment, and I'll be needing a two bedroom apartment for at least a year. Money is no object, because the studio is paying for it, and I'd like to see the ocean. What have you got?"

He rubs his chin while sizing me up. "You say money's no object, huh? Because we have to pay big relocation fees to anyone asked to move before their lease is up."

I don't believe it. He's so sleazy that at the mention of money, he jumps right up for the bait. I know that April's paying around eighteen hundred a month for her apartment, so I've got some idea of what to dangle in front of his face. "Listen, the studio is giving me an allowance of three grand a month for an apartment and a ten grand moving bonus, so just let me know what you've got and when I can get it, and we can do some business. No questions asked."

He looks at me like I'm too good to be true. "Well, I may have just what you're looking for. Will a third floor or a high second floor do? I've got two corner units that are coming up soon, and we're now in the process of negotiating the relocation fees."

This is really interesting, because from what April told me, there's no money for moving out early – only the avoidance of criminal prosecution for dog droppings. This guy's obviously got some scam going to make extra money at the tenants' expense. Now all I have to do is prove it, and April will be off the hook, as will her 'senior citizen' neighbors upstairs, who are sadly only about six years older than me.

He hands me his business card and tells me to check back with him in the next week or so. All that's on the card is his name 'David Miller' and a phone number.

Considering the high amount of her rent and how much April must eat to maintain that frame of hers, she must make pretty good money working for the phone sex company. Boy, if those lonely, desperate, horny guys only knew who was on the other end of the line, I'll bet that would change their mood. I've seen some of the newspaper ads for those

37

sex lines, and it's amazing that men calling in really believe they're talking to the girls in the pictures instead of girls who look like April.

Back at the boat there's a note on my desk, telling me that I have an appointment at the Venice Soundstage on Boccaccio Street, to meet with a man named Joe Caulfield. He's April's boyfriend, and we're supposed to discuss her legal fee.

Just as I'm leaving the boat, the phone rings and I see Stuart's number on my caller ID display.

"Hey Stu, what's up?"

"I just got back from the East Coast, and this time I may have stumbled onto the greatest moneymaking opportunity of a lifetime."

"That's great, Stu, but I'm just leaving the boat for an appointment. Let's get an early bite, and you can tell me all about it."

I knew this would be happening some time around now. Stuart hasn't come up with anything new for almost seven months now and he's definitely behind schedule.

The Venice Soundstage is in a small nondescript building on a side street off of Abbot Kinney Boulevard, and there is no sign outside giving any indication that it's connected to the entertainment industry. This is quite common in Venice, because from what I've been told, everyone from Julia Roberts to Governor Schwarzenegger has a business, office, loft, or residence in this neighborhood, and they all like to keep as low a profile as possible. (Except for 'Arnold,' with his restaurant *Schatzi* on Main Street).

Inside, there's a small office in front and then a five-foot wide hallway that leads back to a four-foot wide door with a small window in it. Peering through, I see that there's a small soundstage in there, complete with quite a few lights on stands and hanging from the high ceiling, cameras on tripods, and lots of cable on the floor connecting everything together. The walls are covered with some dark gray sound-absorbing foam, and when opening the big door and walking in, I'm surprised to see that the set they're using looks just like a courtroom.

Someone finally notices me and walks over. When I tell her I'm there to meet with Joe Caulfield, she tells me that he's the associate producer and points him out to me. I'm surprised to see that he's not huge like his girlfriend is. He's not white like her either. When I tell him who I am, he calls me aside and we walk out the back door of the soundstage to the alley, for some privacy.

"Thanks for coming by Mister Sharp. I really appreciate what you're doing to help out April. She's a sweetheart, isn't she?"

Here's an attractive black guy who's in the entertainment business. When first looking around the soundstage I saw several good looking slender young starlets, both white and black, but he prefers big April. Go figure.

"Yes, she's very nice. My office manager said you wanted to discuss her fee. I told April to talk to her about it, but then was sent over here. What's on your mind?"

"As you can see, we're doing some scenes here that are supposed to take place in a courtroom. Unfortunately, the screenwriter doesn't know a thing about the law or trial procedures, and the only thing we know is what we learned by watching O.J.'s trial. What I'm trying to say is, we're badly in need of a real lawyer as a consultant on this film. Ordinarily, we'd pay about a thousand dollars for some lawyer to advise us for a couple of days, but since you're helping out April, I can arrange to have you put on for the whole five weeks of shooting. If you go through the entire script and keep our film looking as authentic as show business allows, I can arrange for you to get about three thousand a week, and you won't have to be here more than an hour or so each day."

This is interesting. I didn't know that I'd have to take another job just to get paid for April's legal fee, but considering the fact that this assignment will be an interesting one that might produce about fifteen grand, he's definitely got my attention.

"Whatta ya say, Mister Sharp? Are you going to come on board with us?"

The deal is done. We go back inside, Joe has some young big-busted production assistant give me a script to read, and we shake hands. On the way out, I give my business card and social security number to another bimbette and head back to the Marina, now a proud member of the entertainment industry.

The script is definitely not a *Witness for the Prosecution* or *Twelve Angry Men*. In fact, it's so predictable and lacking in plot twist that I wonder why they're even wasting their time and money making it. Every idea in the film has been done before, and there's no difficulty figuring out way in advance how it will end, what the verdict will be, and why.

I've heard that in this town everything depends on who you know, so I guess the producers of this turkey must know some really connected people. After reading the part about the trial, I can see why they need a consultant. This film makes the same mistakes that all the others do, by having the lawyers prance around in between the counsel tables and the bench. In real courtrooms, that area is referred to as the 'well,' and it's definitely off limits to everyone but the bailiff, unless the judge gives the attorneys permission to approach the bench for a 'sidebar.'

The other big error is that the script calls for one of the attorneys to stand next to the witness stand and badger the person testifying. In a real trial, the only time you can get near a testifying witness is with the judge's permission, and that's only granted on rare occasions.

Aside from that, there are some minor errors in objections being made - and the lawyers testifying. They don't take the witness stand, and if it's not an opening statement or closing argument, all a lawyer is supposed to do is ask questions – not comment on the testimony by arguing with the witness and slipping in new facts.

One part of the script that I can't help them with is where a ballistics expert is brought in to testify, because his testimony uses words that I never heard before. I'm pretty familiar with fingerprint jargon, but bullets are another category. Joe Caulfield told me that I would be responsible for accuracy of the whole courtroom scene, so I'm going to have to learn about that subject. All I now know is what I see the crime lab people do on CSI television shows, like compare bullets for similar markings, to see if they were fired from the same gun. Maybe a trip to Tony the cop's target range with him isn't as out of the question as I thought it was.

Returning to the boat, I see Tony the cop sitting on our dock box. He greets me with the news.

"I've been suspended, and they took my gun."

"You mean the big cannon?"

He opens up his sport coat to show me the .50 caliber long revolver in its shoulder holster.

"Naw, they have no right to take this one. I bought it myself. The one they took back is the 9mm peashooter that was issued to me when I first joined the force."

"I'm sorry to hear that. Did they give you any particular reason?"

"Yeah, it's because of that fruitcake shrink. He complained that I threatened him with my gun."

"That's interesting, because the only time you showed him the gun was when he was out on the ledge. In order to turn you in for that, he'd have to admit that he was out on the ledge."

"Yeah you're right, but he says he knew I was coming to see him, so his being out on the ledge was a special psychological test he designed for me. Anyway, this time my leave of absence is without pay, so if you need any detective work done, you know where my boat is."

I sure hope that my urging the shrink to sign Tony's certificate didn't have anything to do with his decision to drop a dime on Tony, because this cop is definitely one guy who I don't want to have mad at me. I board the boat and use my special method of originating a dogmail. One of the cabinets over our sink contains a box of hard dog biscuits. All I have to do is take out the box and shake it a little. Bernie hears the familiar sound of his food rattling, and immediately appears at my feet. While I hand him a biscuit, I tuck a note in his collar, letting the little princess know that Tony's available for investigation assignments.

As usual, the kid is two steps ahead of me. She already knows about Tony's suspension, and an email from her tells me that the dog has been sent over to Tony's boat to give him a new assignment. He's now working on April's case. By the way she's spending money to investigate the manager of April's apartment building, I now realize that the fee I'm getting for being a legal consultant on the film won't belong entirely to me. Now it's a firm matter – a house account.

When I first signed on as the adult part of our law firm, our deal provided for me to share any outside fee with the office only if it entailed the office's assistance in advancing fees, investigation, or other services. Anything I did outside on my own was mine to keep in full. Ever since then, the kid spends almost full time figuring out how to turn my outside work into 'firm' matters, so that she can glom onto part of the fee, and it looks like once again she's succeeded in getting her hooks into me.

My only consolation today is in knowing that she won't get part of my dinner. Stuart is picking up our dinner tab tonight over at the Charthouse Restaurant, while he's trying to lure me into his business deal.

Stuart's Lincoln Town Car pulls up, and from my seat at the bar I can see him waddle into the restaurant. It seems like he adds about twenty pounds for every new business he starts. After we've had a cocktail or two, our table is ready and we order our dinner. Stuart can't resist any more. He starts out. "Peter, you are now looking at number 579."

"What is that Stuart, the amount of pounds you intend to weigh by the end of the year?"

"Oh contraire, mon frer, that is my West Coast code number. It's the number I have to say when calling in to my California broker."

" So, what have you got going now, some stock scam?"

"Not really. I'm betting on baseball, and 579 is my account number with the local bookie I'm using."

"That's it? That's the new business deal you're so excited about? You're now a professional gambler? Stuart, I'm surprised at you. You should know better than that. You can't win in the long run. The odds are against you."

"Uh-uh, Pete. That's where you're wrong. The odds are with me. I can't lose."

"Oh boy, that's great. You'd better hope that they don't hear about your sure-fire winning plan in Las Vegas, because if they do, they'll probably send a chartered plane for you. They love people with systems up there, especially people like you, who have plenty of money."

"Peter, you know me better than that. I'm a conservative businessman. This is a plan that's got real math to back it up."

"Stuart, please spare me the details. You'd be better off trying to invent some perpetual motion machine. Come to think of it, you may have, because planning on winning by gambling is a perpetual loss machine."

"All right, that's enough tearing me apart. Listen, here's the plan, and when you hear it, you'll realize how simple it is.

"Last week I flew up to New Jersey to meet with my car supplier, you know, Billy Z. Well, before I left, I told Vinnie to try and get me down for five hundred on the Dodgers-Mets game. I never heard from Vinnie, so when I got to Billy's office, I told him I wanted to bet on the game. He vouched for me and turned me on to his New York connection. This guy told me that if I wanted to bet on the Dodgers, he could give me seven-to-five odds. I took it, and bet five hundred on the Blue Team.

"The next day, I finally got hold of Vinnie. As usual, he and Olive screwed up my instructions completely, and they bet five hundred of my money out here in California on the Mets. But here's the good part: strangely enough, the odds were the same – but the other way. They got seven to five too.

"Now you know that normal baseball games can't end in a tie, so stop for a second and look at the arithmetic of what happened. I can't win on both bets, so that means I've gotta lose five hundred bucks on one of the bets. But, by the same token, I'm also guaranteed to win seven hundred bucks on the other bet. That means I'm guaranteed a winning spread of two hundred, no matter who wins."

Something is wrong here. Not only am I actually understanding what Stuart is telling me, but it sounds logical.

"Wait a minute, Stu, you mean to say that the bookies know that the odds are different on each coast, but they each take your bets anyway?"

"Sure they do. In fact, they probably lay off money between each other in the same way. Bettors act on emotion. Bookies act on business. When teams are evenly matched, you can almost always get odds against your home team's victory by placing your bet on them in the other team's town. That's because home teams are such favorites with the local fans. All you have to do is find out what the spread is, and establish a line of credit with the bookies. Billy Z took care of my New York connection, and I've got a woman's clothing salesman out here that makes book in the merchandise mart. The only down side is that I'm limited to a thousand dollars a game, so all I can make is an average of about one or two hundred on each. But there are so many hundreds of games going on a year, I can probably pull in over a hundred and fifty grand each season."

"That's nice Stu, but what are you going to do about the income tax?"

"Ah, I knew you were going to ask that. I asked each of the bookies to pay me by money order, so every cent that comes in will be reported on my return."

"What about the payments?"

"Even better. The clothing salesman will accept my check and Billy Z will pay the New York bookie. He'll let me reimburse him by adding the extra amounts onto the car purchases I make from him.

"Every penny that comes in and goes out will be reported to the IRS, and they can audit me any time they want to."

He did it again. Stuart is absolutely the most amazing person I've ever met when it comes to figuring out ways to make money. I only can see one hole in his entire plan. If he gets called in for an audit by the IRS, as I'm sure he will when they see 'gambling' as a listed source of income on his return, he'll have to name his betting connections, which will no doubt lead to audits of the California guy, Billy Zee, and the New York bookie.

I've never been involved with the gambling community, but I have a strong feeling that they won't like getting arrested, audited, and sent to prison for illegal bookmaking operations and federal income tax evasion. I hope Stuart makes a lot of money with his plan, because he may have to hire quite a few bodyguards next year.

Walking down to our boat on C4200 dock after an educational, complimentary early dinner, I see Tony the cop sitting on our dock box again. He hands me a small envelope.

"Here's the info on that cell phone number you gave me."

"Thanks, Tony. By the way, do you know anything about ballistics?"

"All I know is that without me, those experts would be out of work. Why, you got some problem with a bullet?"

"No, it's just this movie I've been brought in on as a legal consultant. They've got a part where some ballistics expert is called to the witness stand. The rest of the witnesses are mostly cops."

"I can't help you with the ballistics part, but I sure can straighten you out about how the cops testify. All I know about bullets is what I've learned from reloading my own."

"You mean you reuse your bullets?"

"Sure. The new .50 caliber ammo for this revolver can cost up to three bucks each. If I go to the firing range three or four times a month, that can cost me several hundred a month. By reloading, I cut that cost down by around two-thirds."

"What do you have to do, pour in some more powder and put a new bullet head on?"

"Yeah, I wish it was that easy. Actually, I use a single-stage center-fire metallic press, with a separate powder measure and a hand-priming tool. The press sits on a ledge in my boat near a portlight. Maybe you've seen it there when passing by my slip."

"Oh, yeah, I did happen to notice it. I thought it was a special device you used to make coffee with. What's involved in reloading ammunition? Is it a complicated process?"

"Not really. There are only five steps. Clean and lubricate the press, resize and decap the cases, re-prime the cases, charge the cases with powder, then seat the bullet in and crimp it. Actually, it's not that hard. I've even taught your little Suzi how to do it. She saw the press and wouldn't leave me alone until she knew how it worked. Hope you don't mind my giving her lessons. She wants to go to the range with me too, but I told her she's a little small for that, and she'd have to get your permission first. About the only thing she could fire that wouldn't push her back onto her rear end would probably be a little .22 caliber pistol."

Okay. So he doesn't know anything about ballistics – just how to recycle killing tools and teach my little roommate the skill. I know that the kid feels like we still owe him for his previous and possibly future help on our cases, so maybe I can get him a job with coaching the movie cops in testifying, especially if I tell Joe Caulfield that Tony will work for less than a thousand a week. That's the easy part. Now it's time for the tough question.

"Would you have any problem working for a black guy?"

"Not at all. Is it a job about coaching actors to testify like cops? Because if it isn't, I'm not interested in being a rent-a-cop working as a security guard."

"Wait a minute, Tony, I thought you were supposed to have some reputation as not caring for black people. Is that only when you're on active police duty, and doesn't apply when you're on suspension?" He's a little surprised by my assessment of his feelings.

"Hey, wait a minute. I have nothing against any person just because of the color of his skin. It's certain cultures that I'm not happy with. We were at war with Germany and Japan just fifty years ago, and now we all drive German and Japanese cars and count them as our allies and our friends. Some blacks were forced into slavery over a hundred and fifty years ago, and hundreds of thousands of white soldiers died in a civil war to help them gain freedom, but every time you see some loudmouth opportunist like Jesse Jackson on television, he's got his hand out for the poor black people who are being discriminated against.

"Well, my question to him is, who's holding guns to the heads of black kids and forcing them to drop out of school? And how does their dropout rate compare to that of Japanese kids? It's not the color of their skin that's doing 'em in, it's their culture.

"I'll bet that when you were a kid, one of your parents read a book to you once in a while, or a nursery story. And they probably also told you to obey the law, stay in school, go to college, and become a useful member of society. Do you think that black kids in the ghetto are getting read to, or being told to stay in school, or helped with their homework? I don't think so, and that's what I don't like. I didn't like school at all, but if I missed a day and my father found out about it, I was in for a beating.

"If someone can show me that they have a respect for other people's rights, and for the law, then I've got no problem with them. If they can't, then they deserve whatever they get. Remember, it wasn't a white guy who walked into that Mexican restaurant to hold it up and probably kill everyone there. I didn't go out of my way to hurt him. He brought it on by himself.

"Now who's this black guy I might be working for, and where's the job?"

He sure set me straight. I guess you can't judge a book by its reputation. Maybe Tony has been getting a bum rap, but being predisposed to dislike any culture is not a healthy way to look at people. I tell him I'll try to get him the job, but I also realize that we can never be close friends.

Back on the boat, I open the envelope he gave me, and see that the cell phone number of the guy that's been bugging Olive is registered to a Hershel Belsky in Beverly Hills. Okay Hershel, it's nice to meet you.

5

I like it when there's some action going on. The few irons I have in the fire this month aren't exactly high profile capital murder cases, but there's still enough to keep my interest level up.

Aside from Olive's Hershel, there's April's crooked apartment building manager, and my budding career in the entertainment industry. April left a message for me that she actually did go out and get one of those pooper-scoopers on a pole, so I feel good knowing that I made an honest woman out of her. Olive hasn't heard from Hershel in a while, so I've still got some time to set up a surprise for him, and I've already got a nice one in mind. I told the kid to have Tony check him out a little more.

And as far as Tony's job is concerned, Joe Caulfield wants to meet with him. He's already agreed with my suggestion to bring in a technical consultant on the cop testimony part of the script, so now it's just a matter of the two of them seeing eye to eye. I've set up a meeting for them on the soundstage. I hope Tony doesn't shoot him until the movie is finished, or at least until I've been paid.

I give Tony my copy of the script to read, so he can see what the movie cops are supposed to testify about.

April is nervous because someone slipped a manila envelope under her apartment door, and she doesn't know what's in it or who left it there. I'm glad she called me before touching it. I tell her to leave it on the floor and that someone from my office is on the way over there. I send Tony over to her apartment and give him instructions to make sure he wears the proper gloves when he picks it up to put it into an evidence bag.

Victor Gutierrez is a friend of mine who operates a private scientific lab out near Pasadena, where he does all types of forensic examinations, from autopsies to fingerprints. After giving Tony directions to Victor's place, I make a phone call so that Tony's arrival will be expected. I want to know everything I can about whoever put that envelope under her door.

Tony's an organized guy. After dropping off the envelope at Victor's place, he calls to check in with me.

"Tony, did you get that thing over to Victor's place?"

"Yeah, but you didn't tell me what he does in the back room."

"Oh, you mean in the body shop portion of his place?"

"Yeah, you could call it that. It wasn't until I noticed his van parked out in back with the name '1800AUTOPSY' painted on the side that I realized what the place was. This guy Victor's been around for years. I've seen him plenty of times when he was doing some consulting work for the department. Oh, by the way, I peeked inside that envelope."

"Anything interesting?"

"Well, that depends on what you consider interesting. It's a couple of eight-by-tens of a dog dumping on a sidewalk. This must be a joke of some sort that someone's playing on her."

Tony doesn't know it, but he just gave me some important information. It looks like that apartment manager is trying to put the pressure on April to move out, so he can get his new tenant moved in. Now that the proof of April's lawbreaking is out in the open, we might as well put an end to her fear of prosecution. I call April.

"Hi, it's attorney Peter Sharp. Can you meet me at your local police station in an hour? I'm going to turn you in for breaking the law."

"Oh, my goodness. Why are you doing this to me? You're supposed to be on my side. You're my lawyer. I don't want to go to jail."

"April, please trust me. You're not going to jail. The worst thing that could happen is you might get issued a citation, like a parking ticket, and then there will be a fifty-dollar fine. Oh, by the way, bring some things with you – Charlie, your new scooper," and your checkbook."

She's not too happy about my suggestion, but she reluctantly agrees to go along with meeting me there.

Victor has my cell phone number, and he's calling me while I'm on the way to meet April at the cop house.

"What's up Victor?"

"I got some prints off of the envelope, and some off of the art photos too."

"Oh, you like those shots do you? I can get some enlargements made that would be suitable for framing, or some wallet sized ones."

"Naw, thanks anyway Pete, I'll stick with my collector's version of those dogs playing poker. Anyway, I just wanted to let you know that the prints we lifted don't match anything on file with the authorities, so whomever they belong to doesn't have a criminal record or any kind of professional license. Have you got anything you want me to compare them to?"

I think about it for a second or two and then remember that the apartment building manager gave me his business card.

"Yeah, come to think of it... I'll be sending a business card over to your place, for comparison. Maybe we'll get lucky."

I'm glad the conversation is over, because I'm just pulling up to the police station, and this town has an ordinance that prohibits talking on a cell phone while you drive. I see through the front doors of the station that April is already here. She's hard to miss.

Walking into the station, I see that she's got Charlie on a leash, and she brought the extended pooper-scooper with her, like I instructed.

The desk sergeant is a friendly sort. "What can I do for you folks?"

I hand him my card. "I'm here with my client, and she wants to confess to a violation of one of your city regulations: Code Section 4.04.385."

The sergeant rubs his chin while looking at me. He thumbs through his desk reference book. "You mean the dog dropping law?"

"Yes sergeant, that's the one. As you can see, my client might have had some difficulty in obeying it in the past, but she's seen the error of her ways and has now purchased this extended scooper, which she religiously uses whenever taking her dog for a walk."

The sergeant is deep in thought. "I'll tell you what counselor, why not write your client's name on the back of this business card you gave me. I'll tell this story to our City Attorney, and if they want, we'll issue her a citation and mail it to her in care of your office. Honestly though, in view of your straightforwardness and coming in here like this, I'm sure that they won't mind letting her off with a warning, this time."

That's it. April's problems are almost over. Mister Miller doesn't know it, but he no longer has anything he can threaten April with. The police already know about her alleged violations of the law.

I'm busy all the way back to the Marina planning the next step, and it involves me making a call to my ex-wife Myra, the newly elected District Attorney of our County.

Back at the boat, I use my office phone to speed-dial her office. Because I was instrumental in convincing her main opponent to drop out of the race, she feels a small debt of gratitude to me, but it doesn't extend any further than the granting of access to her without going through a bunch of office underlings. I have the number of her private line.

"Hello Peter, what favor am I going to refuse today?"

"You see? Once again you've jumped to a wrong conclusion. I'm calling to do you a favor."

"Just a second, a pig just flew by outside my office window."

"No, really, my love, I've got a 518 for you."

"You can't be serious. You mean section 518 of our beloved Penal Code?"

"That's right, beautiful. Extortion. And if you really want to get technical, we've got him cold on section 523, because he sent her a photo that purports to show her violating the law."

"All right Peter, I want to know one or two things, and your answers better be one hundred percent truthful. Number one, I want to know what the subject of the extortion is, and I want to know the requested consideration for it."

"Okay, here goes. The subject of the extortion is my client's alleged violation of the law, and the requested consideration is her voluntarily giving up the two bedroom ocean view apartment she leases, and surrendering her right to any and all compensation by way of relocation funds."

"Hmmm. Sounds interesting. Maybe we can talk about it."

"Good. Now that there's a possibility we have a real case here, why don't we mull over the details at PM?"

"Oh all right, what the heck. I'll see you there at seven this evening. And Peter?"

"Yes my dear?"

"This is strictly a business meeting. If I find out you've concocted another scheme to try and get into my bloomers, I'm outa there."

I wish she wouldn't have hinted that she's wearing bloomers. It's a turn-on. The 'PM' that she mentioned is a Mexican restaurant named Pollo Meshuga, and it was our favorite margarita place while we were dating and during our marriage.

I haven't gotten any word back from Victor yet about a fingerprint match, because the office sent the manager's card over there less than an hour ago, but I'm pretty sure that Miller's prints will be on there somewhere.

I've got some time to kill before meeting Myra this evening, so I'm now on the way over to the Venice Soundstage.

It looks like they're busy shooting a scene back there on the set, but I see Joe Caulfield is in his office, going over some paperwork. I peek in, not wanting to disturb him.

"Hi Peter, your scenes won't be shot for another day or so, but I do appreciate your stopping by the set."

"I was just curious how your meeting went with Tony, that cop I sent over for you to interview."

"He's a unique individual. He starts work tomorrow."

"That's wonderful. Thanks a lot for putting him on. I'm sure he'll do a good job of making your actors testify like real cops."

"Oh, he's not the consultant... we hired him as an actor. He's got quite an imposing presence, what with his size and demeanor, and if he remembers his lines, I'm sure he'll deliver them like a real cop testifying. We figured why risk losing something in the translation when we can get the real thing?"

"You mean he's got a featured role in your movie? Just like that? Doesn't he have to have some kind of screen actor's guild membership?"

"Don't be silly. This is a low budget non-union production, so 'he don't need no stinkin' SAG card.' We can even put you in the movie as one of the lawyers if you want. How about it? Wanna be a star?"

Of all the things in the world that I'm not interested in being, movie actor is right at the top. For the life of me, I can't imagine why people from all over the world gravitate to California for some chance to be in the movies. There must be tens of thousands of wannabee actors out here, and the odds of any of them making it big in the movies is probably worse than their chance of winning the lottery.

If you want a screenplay or an actor, all you have to do is go into any Los Angeles restaurant. Every waiter has a screenplay in the trunk of his car, and the waitresses are all in between acting jobs.

Some of them actually make it, because if you ever watch those celebrity interviews, it seems like every one of them waited on tables at one time in their life. That's where we differ: I've never waited on tables, have never written a screenplay, and do not want to be in the movies. Therefore, I respectfully decline Joe Caulfield's generous offer of fame and fortune, and leave the acting to Tony the cop.

Back at the Marina I see Tony leaving our boat.

"I understand that you're now going to be a movie star, Tony."

"Yeah, isn't that something? You know, that guy Joe Caulfield is a lot smarter than he looks."

"You mean for a guy with black skin? What impressed you about him? Discovering that he can read and write?"

"Very funny, but that's not it. We were discussing various police procedures, and there's nothing I could mention that he didn't seem to already know about - even the different methods of suspect interrogation. He knew about all of 'em, including the Hypothetical Story, the Psychological Approach, the Cold Shoulder, Who Talks First, Playing Down the Offense, Mutt & Jeff..."

"Wait a minute. What's Mutt & Jeff? Two cops of different sizes?"

"Close. That's the technical description for the good-cop, bad-cop routine. He knew 'em all. He doesn't need a consultant on that stuff. He must've had some law enforcement training in his past."

"Or probably some experience working on cops and robber movies. Well, that's neither here nor there. The important thing is that you've got a steady job now for the next couple of weeks, and that the two of you seemed to have gotten along."

"How do you know we got along?"

"Because I just left his office. He's black, and still alive."

"By the way counselor... can he really read and write?"

That's a surprise. Tony the cop actually has a sense of humor. It may be a little on the sick side, but it's still there. In a show of gratitude for getting him the job, he offers to buy me dinner at that same Mexican restaurant we went to last time. I take a rain check that I never intend to cash. There's less chance of gunfire tonight with Myra, although you never can tell what mood she'll be in.

Pollo Meshuga is in a building that looks like a Japanese Pagoda. That's probably because they took the location over after a Benihana restaurant moved out.

As usual I'm at least thirty minutes early, so when Myra comes in, her favorite flavored Patrón margarita is waiting on the table. Because this place is a walking distance from my boat, there's no need to drive and no need to abstain, so I've already had a few and am feeling no pain. I always like to anesthetize myself a little when Myra is around. It eases the pain of her sharp criticism.

I see her come in the front door and she looks as good as ever, but in a more conservative way. No more flaming red hair waving around, no more cleavage showing, but still looking good. Her hair is a conservative darker color, her blouse is buttoned up to a conservative point, and her walk is a little more conservative, on lower more conservative 'sensible' heels and with less motion of the posterior part of her body.

She walks right over to the table, picks up her glass, and with a clink onto mine, takes her first sip. Being a high-ranking Los Angeles County official, a car and driver have been assigned to her, so she doesn't have to worry about drinking and driving any more.

After ordering, we spend a while catching up on mutual friends. Because we're both involved in the law, we know the same people. She doesn't ask about Suzi, who idolizes her, because I think they talk on the phone every day at least once or twice. As a result of Myra, Suzi plans on going to law school and becoming attorney general of the state. I'd like to think they also spend some time talking about me, but there's no sense in getting my hopes up. We both know that Suzi's grand scheme is to get us back together again, so that she can live with a mother and a father. In some ways I wish her luck, but I know in my heart that Myra's had enough of me to last for a lifetime. It looks like the chances of Suzi succeeding are like the punch line of a pit boss in Vegas that I once represented: slim and none.... and Slim's out of town.

We've run out of small talk and now Myra wants more details on the extortion case I mentioned this afternoon. I start right at the beginning and tell her everything I know about April's case. To interest her a little more, I also include the details of Olive's problems with Hershel the car dealer. Maybe she'll take both of them on. Myra listens to it all, orders another drink, finishes up the one still on the table, and gives me her honest opinion.

"Are you out of your frigging mind? What kind of pervert are you? I always knew you were a little kinky when we were married, but this is ridiculous. You've got one phone sex girl referring another phone-sex girl to you. There are two alleged extortion attempts, one for an apartment and another for some dirty talk. You amaze me. I never thought your practice would sink to such depths."

"Hey, wait a minute. What's with that 'kinky' remark? I remember that when we were married you never complained when we played 'the handyman and the housewife.' And if my memory serves me correctly, you came up with a few new versions of that game yourself."

Her face turns a deep red.

"Okay, maybe I was a little harsh with you, but Peter, please, you can't be serious about these cases can you? I know you can do better than turning these losers over to me. I'm going to give you the benefit of the doubt and assume that this was all a ploy just to have dinner with me."

"That works for me. If you don't want these cases, I'll know that I at least tried. And because this satisfies parts of the kid's plan to hook us up again, I also know that I'll be reimbursed for this evening, so drink and enjoy."

Our repartee is interrupted by the cell phone vibrating in my lap. I sneak a glance down at it and see that the text message display says: "Tony was fired."

The rest of the evening's conversation is taken up by our exchanging stories about Tony the cop. She's heard more of them than me, but I actually witnessed two of them. We both decide that extortion cases or not, the evening didn't turn out too bad. She buzzes her driver to bring the car around and I stumble back to our dock, to meet with the newly unemployed movie star.

As usual, Tony is sitting on the dock box next to my boat. I ask him only one question. "You didn't kill him, did you?"

"We disagreed about how a cop should testify. There was a bit of an argument, and he threw me off of the set."

"What's the matter, didn't he think you were authentic enough playing the part of a cop?"

"He thought I was too authentic. He wanted me to tone it down. I tried to explain to him that after a judge makes liberal rulings like that for some shyster defense attorney, no real cop on the stand would act any different. He said he wanted realism and that's what I gave him."

"Well, as long as he's still alive, maybe there's a chance. Did the 'N' word come up at all in your heated conversation with him?"

"C'mon counselor, I'm not that bad, and you should know it by now."

"Okay, I'll talk to him tomorrow. Maybe I can salvage something. Remember, Tony, this is not Court TV, this is a movie. It's all make believe. It's not supposed to be too authentic. Do you think Arnold Schwarzenegger really came from the future, or that Sylvester Stallone can be a champion boxer? It's a fantasy. That's why they call it *acting* instead of reality. I'll try to smooth things out, but if I can talk him into letting you continue as an actor, please follow the director's instructions."

I get his grumbling acceptance and decide to call it a night. I know that the kid will be waiting for me to report on my dinner with Myra, so I might as well get it over with. She'll probably spend the rest of the evening on the phone with Myra, verifying everything I'm about to tell her now.

The next morning Victor calls to let me know that he matched some of the prints on April's manila envelope to the ones on Miller's business card. No surprise there. Now that Myra's decided not to do my heavy lifting, I'll have to take care of Miller myself.

Jack Bibberman has been doing most of our investigation work for some time now and he's pretty familiar with the Hall of Records, so I give him the assignment of finding out exactly who owns that apartment building where April lives. I may have to go over Miller's head to get some satisfaction. I can't imagine any property owners letting a jerk like that keep his job after they've been formally put on notice about how he's been extorting apartments and money from present and future tenants. Once Miller's been bounced from that job as manager, April should be in pretty good shape, figuratively speaking.

My only two loose ends now are Olive's horny boyfriend Hershel, and trying to get Tony his job back as a movie star. No sense in stalling, so I might as well get over to the soundstage to deal with Joe Caulfield.

I have to give him credit. His composure is professional, even when talking about a guy who allegedly almost ruined his film.

"Peter, I know what you're going to say, but I don't think I can do it. He's just too real, and he can't let it go. I'm sorry to do this to a close friend of yours."

"First of all, he's not a close friend of mine. Other than a certain dock in the Marina, the only thing we share is a common lack of affection for each other. But as for him being too real, I agree. It would probably be like having me in your movie, with the script calling for me to walk around in front of the counsel tables with a lit cigar in my hand. That just doesn't happen in real life... at least not since Clarence Darrow retired. I've already told him that it's make believe, and I feel pretty sure he'll go along with it. Whattaya say? Isn't there some way you can give him another chance? You know, the film doesn't even have to be rolling. You could just make it a rehearsal to see if he'll go along with the program."

Joe looks down at his desk. He's thinking it over. That's a good sign, because it's much better than the quick 'no' that I got when this conversation started. He looks up at me, like he's made a decision.

"You know, I really do want to get him back with the company, because there's another position we could definitely use him for. In addition to film production, we're expanding by starting a bonded and licensed film courier company. There's a big problem with motion picture piracy of newly released movies, and we intend to launch our new service along with the release of our film. Tony would be a good addition to that division, because we want to have armed people delivering major studio films for showing at sneak previews and premiers."

"That's fine, but if you throw him out for his acting, I'm afraid that there'll be too much permanent ego damage for him to accept a lesser position."

"It wouldn't be a lesser position... we're prepared to make him security supervisor of the whole operation. We'll be offering an entirely new service to the motion picture industry, with a security guard present during all showings of the feature films we deliver. They can't knock off the film onto a digital copy unless it's being projected at the theater, and we'll have one of our guys in the projection booth during all showings.

"Tony can be put into a position to do all the hiring and training of the security guards. It'll be his show from day one."

"I don't know, Joe. There's still a chance that he can get reinstated with the police department, and I know that's the job he'd prefer over anything else."

"Peter, he's already been on the force for over twenty years. His pension is vested. If he retires now, he gets a full pension and can still take the job with us. It'll be like a double income, and there'll be no one shooting at him."

"I'll talk to him. Maybe if he sees the whole picture, he'll be more inclined to go along with the acting directions. I think that the loss of the acting job hurt him more than anything else, because he probably told everyone he knows about his being in a movie. When the picture comes out and he's not in it, it'll be a big letdown for a macho guy."

"Okay Peter. You win. First, you let him know about the courier service and get him to agree to go along with the acting direction. Then have him come back to the stage, and we'll do a run-through of his scenes. Maybe we can talk about that other position some time in the future... after he's appeared in the movie."

Mission accomplished.

I've heard of motion picture piracy before, but never knew how serious it was until I did some research on the internet and discovered that a recently released report from the International Intellectual Property Alliance found that the U.S. economy lost an estimated 9.2 billion dollars in 2002 as a result of unlawful copy and sales of our movies. In China, approximately 91% of all movies sold and shown are pirated, and Brazil isn't even a close second, with a piracy rate of only about 50%.

Methods of the crimes range from theft of a print from a theater, tapping into cable TV, and individual VCR copying, to bringing a camcorder into a theater and capturing the movie right off of the screen. And the almost ten billion will certainly grow exponentially when there is enough broadband access to allow peer-to-peer exchange of movies on the internet. I've also heard that some theaters are using special spy devices to detect when someone in the audience is using a video camera to tape a movie while it's being shown on the theater's screen.

Now I'm beginning to understand why Joe Caulfield's company wants to have armed security guards stay with those first-run prints while they're being projected in theaters. There are some reports of bootlegged movies being sold on the streets of China and Brazil before they even reach the movie houses in the U.S. I guess that if the studios can save a couple of billion bucks, it's worth it for them to pay Joe Caulfield's new service to guard their deliveries of prints to theaters for sneak previews and premieres.

It would be almost impossible to guard up to 3,000 prints of a film that goes into wide distribution, but it sure would be nice if they could keep copies of the film off of the streets of China and Brazil until the movie at least has a chance to get to those 3,000 theaters.

Back at the boat, I tell Tony about my meeting with Joe Caulfield, how he can get a second chance at the acting job, and about the new security position available to him.

"I don't know, counselor. It would mean putting in my papers and leaving the force."

"Here's my suggestion, Tony. Why not just go to the stage, meet with Joe, get the acting gig back, and tell him you'll think over his offer about the courier job. That way you can see if your continuing on the police force is an option at all. If it is, then you'll have a decision to make. If it isn't, well, let's cross that bridge when we get to it."

He agrees with my logic and promises to behave himself on the second go-around. Strangely enough, he seems to have made some friends during the short period of time he spent with the film company. He told me that one or two of the production crew also frequent the same target range in Agoura that he shoots at. I guess that shooters share the same mind-set. It's them against all those 'pinkos' who want to stomp on their Second Amendment rights to own a private arsenal.

I remember seeing an old actor named Charlton Heston when he was president of the National Rifle Association. In one rabble-rousing speech before his group, he held a weapon up over his head and declared that if they want his gun, they'll have to take it out of his cold, dead hand. I wonder exactly who he was referring to as 'they?' I certainly never wanted his gun, but I think that when he was diagnosed with Alzheimer's, he should have voluntarily given it up. If you've got a gun in your house that's not for target practice, it's probably to protect against any intrusion by strangers, and to a person with Alzheimer's, even a close friend or relative might be mistaken for a stranger, due to loss of a patient's ability to recognize people. Can you imagine some old guy with Alzheimer's sitting in his room with a loaded weapon on his lap? That's a disaster waiting to happen.

Personally, I have nothing against guns. It's the bullets that scare me.

6

Olive has been calling. She's really upset because 'Hal' has been bugging her to get together, and now he's offering her money to model for him. What a perv.

I return Olive's phone call and give her some instructions. First, she's not to call Hal's cell phone under any circumstances, unless I tell her to. Second, the next time he calls, she's to agree to model for him, but it'll have to be a special way, and she'll call him back with the details.

Olive wants to know what I've got in mind, but I think it's best that she stay out of the loop on this one, because she might not appreciate my method.

I've had Jack B. checking out this Hershel Belsky, and it just hit me: he's got the biggest car dealership in Beverly Hills and does a tremendous amount of television advertising. His commercials are usually shown very late at night, when they run all the old 'B' movies.

I stayed up late a couple of nights ago watching him make a fool out of himself, and he keeps mentioning that pretty soon his dealership will have a 'dream girl' that will act as his spokesperson for the 'dream deals' he makes on his cars. I hope he's thinking what I think he's thinking. That confuses me a little, but I'm calling Olive anyway.

"Hi Mister Sharp, what's up?"

"Olive, I want you to call your friend Hal and tell him that you've been thinking about what he wants you to do. If my guess is right, I think he wants to hire you as the spokesperson for his car dealership."

"You mean you want me to go to work for this creep?"

"No Olive, I don't want you to work for him, I just want you to find out if he'll hire you sight unseen, based on how you describe yourself to him."

"Gee, I don't know...."

"And when you talk to him, please try to use that same voice your trainer taught you. He'll be more amenable to hiring you sight unseen if you can get a rise out of him on the job interview phone call. And don't forget to tell him how beautiful you really are, but remind him that you're not the same girl that your company used in its photo ads."

I hear a beep on my phone, which means there's another call coming in. I make sure Olive has my instructions, and switch to the other line.

"Mister Sharp, I'm a production assistant over at the Venice Soundstage. Joe Caulfield wanted me to tell you to come over here as soon as you can."

This can't mean anything good. I hope Tony hasn't shot anyone over there.

When I get to the soundstage, they're all waiting for me in Joe's office. Joe starts first.

"Peter, we can't allow real loaded guns on the set. Our insurance company specifically put that clause in the completion bond. There are a lot of scenes in the movie where people are shooting guns, and they're all phony, firing caps, to give off a little smoke. We add the actual gunshot sound in post production."

"So? That's what you called me over here for? Some provision in your insurance policy?"

"Not exactly Peter, it seems that our new star is a little temperamental about surrendering his weapon to the prop guy. He insists on wearing that huge thing in his shoulder holster. I admit that it gives a nice touch to the movie because whenever he leans forward the camera can see it in there. Unfortunately though, we can't allow it."

Tony can't sit quiet any longer.

"Did you see what they want me to wear? Some piss-ant .32 caliber revolver with a snub-nosed barrel. And to make things worse, it's not even real. It's a replica!"

Saying this, Tony pulls out the pistol and tosses it over to me. I catch it and take a close look. It feels and weighs like the real thing.

"Tony, this gun is an exact replica of the real thing. What's wrong with your carrying it in the movie?"

"Because counselor, if anyone I knew saw me with that pea-shooter, my reputation would be ruined."

I look around the room at the expressions of frustration on Joe Caulfield, the director, the prop man, and some other above-the-line people seated there.

"Okay, I've got a suggestion. Part of your soundstage is supposed to be the cops' squad room. Why don't you take a camera off of the set and get a shot of Tony putting his real cannon into a desk drawer somewhere, and then slamming and locking the drawer. Then you can cut back to him in the squad room, as he puts on a different shoulder holster with the small revolver in it, while he tells another cop in the room that the judge doesn't want him to bring the big gun into the courtroom. And after the close up of the first desk is shot, I'm sure you can provide some safe place for Tony to lock up the real thing until after his courtroom scene is shot."

They're all looking at each other. Several conversations are going on at the same time between the groups in the room. The camera guys are talking about how to frame the close-up of the desk drawer, the props and wardrobe people are talking about the other cop and what he should be wearing, the continuity guy is conferring with the director about how to continue the scene from outside the set to inside the set, and Joe Caulfield is talking to Tony about the exact dialogue he can live with.

With all those little meetings going on, they don't even notice my walking out of the room. On the way out, Renaldo, the production assistant who called me, introduces himself. He looks a little old to be a production assistant, because he's probably in his late thirties. We chat for a few minutes about how production is going, and he tells me that everyone on the set is afraid of Tony. They know he's a decent guy, but they're still reluctant to say anything that might upset him. I also learn that Ren is the guy that Tony mentioned as being a film crewmember who he went shooting at the target range with.

Ren also tells me about all of the constant arguments that Tony and Joe Caulfield are getting into about dialogue, blocking, character attitude, and just about everything concerning Tony's on-camera scenes. From what I hear, it sounds like there's a constant ongoing feud between Tony and Joe, so I hope Joe stays alive until Tony's scenes are finished. Ren seems like a pretty decent guy, so I decide to take a chance and see if he'll help me out.

"You know Ren, I really want to be kept up to date on how things are going with my friend Tony. Would it be possible for me to retain you on a part-time consultant basis? I'd like to receive a phone call from you every afternoon, with a status report on whether or not Tony has shot anyone on the set, or if anything else out of the ordinary has taken place with him being involved."

Ren seems to be amenable to my consultation job, so I offer him an initial retainer of two fifty-dollar bills and tell him that I'll be straightening out with him at least once a week. The offer is pocketed, and I now have an inside connection in the movie industry.

While I'm here I decide to take a little tour of the various rooms connected to the soundstage. The executives are still in Joe's office working out Tony's new scenes and the rest of the crew is out at the catering truck, so I shouldn't be getting in anyone's way. While I'm between the makeup room and the green room, one of the young starlets sees me walking around and because I probably look like I'm lost, she offers to help me. I can see why there's so much trouble in celebrity marriages. With all this temptation around, it's a wonder that any of them stay married. She asks me if I live in the neighborhood, because she does too, and she hasn't seen me around before.

When I tell her that I live on a boat in the Marina, she excitedly tells me that I'm just like her dad... he likes boats too. She wonders if I know him. I tell her that we probably have met at the Marina in the senior citizens' center. A reality check like this is never welcome, but it brings home the fact that I will never be with a beautiful young starlet unless I'm a big movie star or a producer – and neither of those careers is on my horizon. But I could easily settle for a thirty-six-year-old female District Attorney I know.

I never realized how much is entailed in the production of a movie. The various rooms in this building contain well-lit make-up desks, wardrobe racks, a large area with flat sections of walls that resemble the interiors of different rooms, a prop department with all sorts of things, an editing room with numerous monitors and hi-end video equipment, a camera and grip storage room, and one other that has a 'no admittance' sign on the outside of the door.

Anything sign telling me to keep out of some place invariably becomes a definite invitation for me to go in. That's always been a certainty with guys like me. I try the doorknob and it's open, so I stick my head into the room and look around. This was a waste of my time. There's nothing in the room but a bunch of DVD recorders like the one on my boat, and a machine that I looks like something I've never seen before anywhere but on the bridge of Captain Kirk's Starship Enterprise. I have no idea what it is, but I do see that it some large glass doors on the front, and through them I can see some reels, with what looks like film on them. My guess is that the film goes from one reel, through some other parts of the machine, and then winds around the other reel. All I can see that is recognizable is a small label that identifies this device a 'Rank Telecine.' I don't know what it does other than probably cost a lot of money.

When I pass by Joe's office, everyone else is gone, but Joe is still in a conference with Tony. The absence of gunfire is a sign that everything is under control, so I'm leaving the building. I like to quit when I'm ahead.

Dean Doheny is a friend of mine who works in the advertising business, and I've asked him to see if he can find out anything he can about Hershel's plans to use a spokesperson. I'd like to know if there's any possibility that he has Olive in mind for that position, and if the position will ever exist.

Now that Olive's matter is moving along, I can turn back to April's case and read the report that Jack B. sent in. The building that she lives in is owned by a real estate trust. The two main players in the trust are a Chad and Ruth Sinclair, who live in Holmby Hills, one of the richest parts of town. Jack's search revealed that the Sinclairs own more than just the one building where April's apartment is, they also control several other choice properties with ocean views.

I send a response to Jack, telling him to check out those other properties and see if there's any hanky-panky or under-the-table deals going on with the other managers too.

That's enough work for one afternoon, so I call a cab to take to Mi Ranchito for some Patrón margaritas and a huge custom made burrito, containing everything the house has to offer, including onions, sour cream, tomatoes, shredded lettuce, extra beans, rice, olives and guacamole. When the cook gets that order he knows it's for me, so I usually get it exactly the way I order it.

After a nice evening that includes an extremely filling dinner and drinks, and watching a soccer game broadcast in Spanish, the cab drops me off at the Marina, so I get in bed and continue with my plans to watch late nite television to see what Hershel Belsky has to offer in his car commercials.

The television wakes me at the time I set for it: two in the morning. *The Magnificent Seven* is playing, and there's a gunfight going on between the bandito, played by Eli Wallach, and the seven heroes, played by Yul Brynner, Steve McQueen, Horst Bucholtz, Robert Vaughn, Charles Bronson, James Coburn and Brad Dexter. I know those names by heart and have won quite a few bets in drinking establishment by naming them all correctly. I used to know the names of all Santa's reindeers, and also the Seven Dwarfs and Seven Deadly Sins, but most of the money bets were for those seven magnificent cowboys. If I ever learn the names of every guy Elizabeth Taylor was married to, I could probably make some money in gay bars too.

Just as the scene gets interesting, the movie stops mid-sentence and a commercial for Hal's Beverly Hills Auto Mart flashes onto the screen. Sure enough, there's Hershel doing his spiel. If there was ever a poster boy for male menopause, it's him. He must be pushing sixty, and is riding one of those Segway scooters around on his used car lot, stopping in front of each used reconditioned junk just long enough to pitch it to the viewers. His full head of hair is dyed black, probably with shoe polish. The silk shirt is a regular, with an extra large guy stuffed inside of it, which causes the buttons in front to look like they're about to pop off. The top buttons are left open, giving us a view of his hairy chest and the several gold chains hanging around his neck. His stunning polyester pants are held up by a wide, shiny white belt. Coincidentally, the belt matches his shiny white leather shoes. If you borrow a bartender's reference guide and look up 'night crawler,' you should see a picture of Hershel.

But you have to give credit where it's due and Hershel certainly deserves some. He's obviously a very shrewd businessman who has built a successful new and used car dealership in the heart of America's richest and most famous neighborhood. He sounds like a really good pitchman, and his offer "you get a Segway scooter with the purchase of any new or used car in our inventory" certainly should be tempting for most people.

To preserve his image for posterity, I've got my TIVO running during the commercial. After it's over I go back to the part where he offers that scooter and see that down at the bottom of the screen is a lot of small print that describes the offer in more detail. Even with my huge fifty-two-inch high definition flat plasma screen I can barely make out the tiny print explaining that the Segway is not exactly a gift, but instead is a one month free trial, after which time it can be purchased from Hershel's dealership at some allegedly discounted wholesale price. He's no fool.

While the movie is running I check out that scooter on the Internet and discover that this little 2-horsepower people mover with Michelin tires is controlled by 5 internal gyroscopes and has a gearbox that is sealed and designed to be maintenance free. The specs state that a rider must be between 100 and 250 pounds, so it looks like Hershel is pushing the upper limits.

Suzi rides around the Marina in one of those electrical golf-cart-like devices. If it wasn't for the fact that she won't go anywhere without the beast, a Segway would be perfect for her... as soon as she's big enough to see over the handlebars. The company's specs list an operating range of between 11 to 15 miles on a full charge, and that's much more than the average person would ever walk in a normal day. This means that it's definitely not intended to replace the automobile, but only designed as a pedestrian's aid.

When Hershel's commercials continue, he makes reference to a big event that he'll be hosting at his dealership soon. One of the car manufacturers he represents will be introducing a brand new sporty little convertible to the market. If what he says is true, this must be the project he wants Olive's voice and body for. I'll check with my ad guy Dean Doheny tomorrow to see if I'm in the ballpark with this guess.

Hershel wasn't lying. According to Dean's inside info, Hershel actually is making a big budget commercial, to be shot on film. Hershel's advertising agency sent out copies of the shooting script for some bids on production of the commercial.

From the bits and pieces of information that Dean was able to get, there actually is a brand new sporty little convertible being manufactured in a plant up in northern California. The new car will be rolled out in a month or so, and Hershel has made arrangements with the factory to have the first demo of that model brought down to his dealership so that he can throw a 'premiere' party and offer it to prospective customers for a test drive.

Dean tells me that the auto factory is pitching in the major part of Hershel's advertising budget, and once it gets to his dealership, they'll be doing the same thing with their other dealers in a dozen or so major markets like Chicago, New York, and other big cities.

Someone's knocking on the hull. I look over the rail and see that it's the messenger service guy. He hands me a large envelope and I hand him a buck. The envelope is from Hershel's advertising agency and it's addressed to 'Peter Sharp Productions.' It looks like Dean established a new business for me, and the agency sent a script over for us to bid on it.

Parts of the script look professionally done, but most of the local dialogue definitely shows Hershel's personality, because there are sexual overtones. Everyone including the advertising industry knows that sex sells, but they'd never believe what a big customer Hershel is.

The commercial starts out at the factory, with the new little convertible approaching the end of the assembly line. Some workers are putting on the finishing touches and buffing the shiny paintjob to a high gloss. Two other workers bend down and attach front and rear 'manufacturer' license plates, so the vehicle will be street legal.

Finally, a worker gets into the car and drives it out to the factory's parking area, where an attractive female with a sexy voice tells him "ooh, I like your car. Can I ride in it?" The worker gets out of the car and holds the door open for the female, who slides in behind the wheel and sensuously rubs her hand over the upholstery, while saying "ooh, I like it." It looks a little stupid on paper, but I guess a good director or a genius like Paris Hilton can do something with it.

From what I've read so far, it looks like Hershel wants the girl to give viewers the impression that she'd like to make love to this car. The intended audience is obviously men, who are probably supposed to believe that if they drive a car like this, it will be a 'babe magnet,' and beautiful women will surround them, waiting their chance to stroke the car and its owner. If I know anything about Hershel, the only screwing those customers will ever get is in his sales office.

After the female drives away from the factory, she heads down a long stretch of highway. In the next shot, the camera sees her approaching in the distance, and we see the heat waves coming up off of the highway, much like that famous scene in *Lawrence of Arabia*, where Peter O'Toole is seen riding toward the camera. After another ten seconds of seeing the car approach, there is a 'dissolve,' to the next shot, which shows the female pulling onto Hershel's lot. A wide shot establishes the entire dealership building, and then zooms down to her pulling through the large doors and onto the showroom floor.

While all this driving is taking place, there is a voice-over by the sexy female, letting the viewers know how important it is to have a 'nice, luxurious ride,' and how 'cuddly' the car makes her feel. More hype to make men think that women can't wait to get into this car. When the car finally comes to a stop on Hershel's showroom floor, the female lets out a passionate yell, as if she's just experienced an orgasm, brought about by the sexy feeling of driving this car for the past few hours.

Once again, I have to give Hershel credit. Somehow, he's managed to combine a car commercial with phone sex dialogue. I have no idea whether it will be successful or not, but it certainly will be talked about around every office water cooler the day after it's first aired on television. No wonder he wanted someone like he thinks Olive is to do this commercial.

If what Olive tells me is true, Hershel has created such a strong fantasy about what she looks like, that he wants her to star in the commercial and definitely do the voice over. The script from the agency gives notice to all interested production companies that any person that they cast for the lead is subject to approval by the local sponsor – Hershel. This means that my main task now is to see to it that Hershel is persuaded to hire Olive sight unseen. She's an attractive girl, but doesn't have the drop-dead good looks that I'm sure the advertising agency will be looking for in this commercial.

The ad agency's budget calls for a fee of twenty-five thousand for whatever supermodel does the commercial. With Dean's help, we find out how many production companies are in the bidding, how much the average bid is, and which bidders have the least amount of respect for Hershel. He's been advertising quite a bit over the years and an obnoxious guy like him is certain to have made some enemies around town.

We find out that there are nine production companies bidding and that their estimates are coming in at between ninety and one hundred ten grand. Dean has discovered that there's a production company out there that was screwed over by Hershel in the recent past, so they declined an offer to bid on the project. I find out the name of the boss at that agency and tell him my plan, and that if he wants to bid on this commercial, I can guarantee him that Hershel will approve the lead actress, and that his production company may not have to pay her the full fee budgeted.

This gets the boss' attention. He checks his figures over and calculates that if he were to do this production, his bid would be in the neighborhood of ninety thousand. I let him know that I can get a sponsor-approved star to work for only fifteen thousand, so he can lower his bid to eighty thousand, be the lowest bidder, get the job, and get even with Hershel. He wants to know the form his revenge will be allowed to take, but all I tell him is that it's entirely legal and he'll love it.

So far this sounds like it can be a win-win proposition for everyone involved except Hershel. I call Olive to get the ball rolling. Her first assignment is to call Hal and let him know that she watches his commercials every evening, knows about the new commercial he's doing, and wants him to send her a script, so she can practice the dialogue. She's to promise him that after she's done the dialogue, she'll send him a tape, so that he can approve the voice-over part of the commercial. She's a little hesitant and has some questions.

"What happens if he wants to meet with me? Should I actually see him?"

"Definitely not. We want him to be so excited with the way you sound, that he fantasizes about the way you look. I want you to get him to hire you sight unseen."

"I don't know. He seems like a pretty shrewd guy. You think he'll go for that?"

"Olive, it's up to you to make him go for it. Let me give you another incentive. The advertising agency's budget calls for a nice fee for whoever gets this job. If you can convince Hal to hire you, then you may be in line for over seven thousand dollars."

This definitely gets her attention. After we hash it over for a while, I talk Olive into giving Hershel plenty of excitement over the phone, just like she used to do... and promise him that if she gets the job, there'll be more of the same in the future... more than he could ever imagine in his wildest dreams.

Olive promises to get out her little black book and do a little research. From what she tells me, each one of those phone sex girls keeps records of the customers they talk to and what special pieces of business really turns them on. Olive will be going through her book to see what buttons to press for Hershel.

As I hang up the phone the dynamic duo walks past me. The dog ignores me completely because I'm not eating anything that might drop to the floor. The kid gives me one of those 'what're you up to now?' looks.

Ren calls from the soundstage. Tony and Joe Caulfield had another big argument. I'm glad to hear that no one got fired, and even better, no one got shot. I watch for Tony to return from a hard day of being a movie star. When I see him walking toward his boat, I motion for him.

"I hear you guys were at it again today. Anything serious?"

"Did you give them legal advice on police regulations for giving the Miranda warnings to a suspect in custody?"

"What's wrong, Tony, they wouldn't let you beat a confession out of someone?"

"No, that's not it, but when you've got a suspect in custody and he starts to blurt something out to you that will help with the case, there's no way that we're going to shut him up in the middle of a sentence and say 'wait a minute mister perp, before you say anything, here are some constitutional rights you should be aware of.' It just doesn't work like that in the real world, counselor."

"I never told them to apply the rules like that. I just wanted them to know that once a suspect requests an attorney, the interrogation should stop."

"Well, that's not the way they're doing it. They're giving the suspect more protection than the victim."

"Tony, did you ever see one of the *Terminator* movies?"

"You mean the ones with our esteemed Governor Schwarzenegger?"

"Yes, with Arnold. In each one of those movies, he winds up killing quite a few people. Most of them are bad guys. Do you think that in real life Arnold Schwarzenegger could actually pull the trigger and shoot people?

"And in every one of those television shows on law and order, there's someone who has killed someone else. They're not killers in real life either.

"You've got to separate real life from the movies. What people see you do in the movies is completely different from what you would do in a similar situation in real life. That's why they call it acting. Let me ask you a question. Did you ever get a chance to read the screenplay all the way through? I mean past just the scenes that you're in?"

Silence. There's no answer from him on that question.

"I thought so, because if you did, you'd see that the guy gets convicted anyway, due to some new evidence that comes in, and a new eye witness they discover who was out of town for the first part of the trial."

"He does? You mean the guy actually goes down for the crime?"

"Yes. Don't you see? They want to make it look like the bad guy is going to win. That's why his liberal lawyer's objections are always getting sustained by the liberal judge. In the movie business, they call that a plot 'hook,' to set up a surprise ending for the audience.

"So, now that you know you'll win in the end, can you please just go along with the script? By the way, did Joe Caulfield tell you about the film courier service he wants you to run?"

"Yeah, he mentioned it. And you're right. I'll try to keep my opinions to myself on the set, but boy, that Joe sure gets on my nerves."

Olive calls to let me know that she spoke to Hal. They had a long conversation, and she feels pretty sure that he was locked in his private bathroom during the entire time they were talking. He promised to send her a script by messenger, so tonight she'll start practicing her lines. I call Joe Caulfield, to make arrangements for Olive and I to use the soundstage's voice-over booth to make a recording tomorrow evening, after everyone else has quit for the day.

Dean calls to let me know that the production company I talked to put in their bid to do the commercial, and that the advertising agency is considering going with them because they bid less than everyone else by almost ten thousand dollars. Good. It's all starting to come together now.

Another phone call comes in from the production company. They want to thank me for giving them a heads-up on the bidding, and to make sure that they'll be able to keep up their end of the bargain. What they're really looking for is some assurance that their lead actress will be approved by the sponsor and that per my promise, she'll work for the fifteen thousand that they budgeted for.

I put them at ease by letting them know that everything's going along according to plans, and to keep me up to date on when they plan to start shooting. I also tell them that all the voice-over work is being done in another studio, so all they'll have to do is lay it in at the right spots when they do their post-production editing.

They're pleased to hear this, because it means they just saved thousands of dollars in sound booth rentals and engineering.

Olive and I make a date to meet at the soundstage tomorrow evening to rehearse her lines. I borrow a digital tape recorder from one of our dock neighbors and practice using it for a while until I get used to pressing the right buttons. The production company assured me that their equipment works with this tape format.

Jack B. calls to give me some news on the April apartment building project. He discovered that D. Miller, the manager at April's building, is also the manager at several of the other buildings owned by that real estate trust controlled by the Sinclairs. Jack will be conducting some interviews with the tenants at those other properties.

I still don't have an idea finalized as to how to handle the owners and that Miller guy, but after Jack finishes up his investigation, I'm sure some way will become clear. While I sit here dreaming up new strategy, I hear a strange noise. I'm afraid it's the boat's engines being started up.

This is a noise that is not pleasant to me. The sound itself isn't what bothers me, it's the fact that if the engines are running, that means the boat may be moving soon. I see the kid moving around working switches on a control panel, revving the engines, and giving orders to the four Asian Boys who always seem to be around whenever she needs something done. They do maintenance work on most of the boats here on our dock, and I also see them working as waiters and busboys at the Chinese restaurant around the corner, where Suzi's late mother worked, and where the kid is treated as a celebrity.

I hear her shouting out some orders, and the Boys are running around on the dock, loosening the dock lines and making sure that the boat doesn't bump into the pilings that support the dock.

In the past, whenever there was some reason to move the boat, I would go up to the flybridge and be a 'shill' for the kid, who really knows how to drive this thing. She would do the work from the lower steering station, and I would pretend to be in charge.

This time, it's almost sunset and no one is watching us, so we don't have to do our act. I'm just going to sit here on the couch and relax while she does whatever she has to do. I've been informed by other boaters that you have to actually take these things out of the slip every once in a while, just to give the engines some exercise. This time, I think that the kid wants to take the boat out at least three miles past the breakwater so that she can flush out the holding tanks.

Whatever she wants to do is okay with me, as long as I don't have to learn how to drive this thing. I enjoy living on it, but have no fascination with boats that actually move. At first I thought she might have difficulty in locating our slip when she returns here after dark, but now I realize that what the Asian Boys were painting on the tops of the two pilings yesterday was actually a glow-in-the-dark paint. This means that returning to the slip later this evening, those two glowing tips will be visible almost a mile away.

At first I felt a little guilty in not being able to drive this boat, but that feeling subsided whenever I looked over to George Clooney's megayacht. I believe with all my soul that he couldn't drive that thing if his life depended on it. That huge ship of his is almost three times the size of this one, and we have a crew of four just to handle the lines and pull up the fenders on this one. And once our boat gets back to the slip, they're all quite busy re-tying the dock lines and hosing the boat down to get the saltwater off of it. I have a feeling that George does just what I'm doing. He sits back and enjoys other people driving the boat and doing all the work. I knew we had something in common.

Just as we pull out of the slip my cell phone rings. It's Ren calling from the soundstage. They're through shooting for the day, but Tony and Joe Caulfield are still in the office fighting over tomorrow's shooting script. I tell Joe that from now on, the only time he should feel compelled to call and check in with me is when someone actually gets shot – by Tony.

Surprisingly, the cruise is quite enjoyable. Our main tourist attraction in the Marina is called Fisherman's Wharf, and its phony New England fishing town waterfront design is attractively lighted in the evening. I've never seen it from the water at night before, and it's a very nice sight. It's a bit bumpy leaving the harbor and going around the breakwater, but once the kid flicks another switch, a device called 'stabilizers' kick in, and the rolling motion stops.

The only slight problem I have with going out past the breakwater is getting seasick. There've been plenty of theories about what causes seasickness, but I think I've finally got the right answer. It's the same thing that can get to you when you're reading in a moving car. It's not necessarily the motion that can make you feel nausea coming on, it's the sensory conflict that you pick up because of a difference in motion between your primary senses of vision and motion. In a moving car, when you try to read, your close focus is on a stationary object, the item you're reading, while your peripheral vision is picking up the motion of scenery whizzing by the car window. This sensory conflict can get to you.

The same thing can happen on a boat, but instead of your peripheral vision sensing motion, it's your inner ear feeling the motion of the boat. The conflict occurs when you're close focused on some part of the boat that's moving with you, so it appears to be standing still with respect to your body. Every person has his or her own tolerance level. I remember one time a guest on our boat asked me to close the blinds on some windows because she was starting to feel woozy while we were sitting still in the slip. Evidently she was looking out our windows and saw the boat moving up and down ever so slowly, in contrast to the nearby apartment buildings.

I guess the only way to combat the feeling is to keep all three of your motion senses lined up - close focus, peripheral vision, and inner ear. The only way to do this is to look out in the distance so that you can see the exact same motion that you feel. This works for me. All that a seasickness drug like Dramamine does is dull your senses, so that they might ignore the conflict. Personally, I'd rather have my senses about me and avoid seasickness the natural way.

Suzi reaches a place that is supposed to be at least three miles out and then turns back toward land, presenting us with another nice view of the West Los Angeles coastline. As planned, she has no problem finding the slip, and soon the engines have been turned off. Once the Asian Boys have the boat secured, quiet resumes.

If I can avoid getting sick, going to sea always makes me hungry and thirsty, so I call a cab and make plans to once again become a drunken sailor at Mi Ranchito.

Olive succeeded in getting hired sight unseen. She must have really laid it on thick to Hershel, because the production company called to ask me when their featured actress would be available for a rehearsal. They planned on a three-day shoot. One day up in Northern California at the factory, one day on the highway, and ending up at Hershel's dealership for the live telecast of his 'premiere' of the new car.

I told them that I'd bring the dialogue to them on a digital tape, and they said that I shouldn't be worried about timing. As long as all the dialogue is on the tape, they'll put it in the commercial at the right places and mix it in with the music they'll be adding.

Olive calls.

"Hi Mister Sharp, it's Olive. When Hal told me I was hired, he gave me the name and address of the production company that's shooting the commercial. I'm supposed to go over there for a rehearsal. Are you coming with me?"

"No Olive, I'm not going to be there with you."

"Oh, okay. I just thought you'd like to… oh, never mind. When do you think I should go over there? Hal said they'd be expecting me to call."

"Olive, I'll tell you about it tonight, when we make your dialogue recording at the Venice Soundstage."

As arranged, Olive arrives right on time at the soundstage this evening. Everyone has already gone home, but I paid Ren to stay a little later to help us set up the microphone. It's a good thing that the session is this evening, because Ren tells me that it's the only night he has off from his other job. I don't ask him any personal questions, because one of the other crewmembers mentioned one time that he works evenings as a projectionist at a local movie theater.

Olive surprises me. Using her best phone sex voice, she goes through the several sentences flawlessly and really makes it sound alluring. Hershel will definitely be getting his money's worth out of this soundtrack. Now I can see how Olive made such a nice living doing that conversational business... she's really good at it.

After she's all done, I tell Ren that it's a wrap, and he closes up the stage, handing me the recorder to return to our dock neighbor. I take the digital cassette and put it in a messenger bag to be sent to the commercial production company tomorrow.

Olive sees me putting the tape into the bag.

"You don't have to spend any money sending the tape over to the production company, Mister Sharp. I'm planning on going over there tomorrow morning and I can deliver it for you."

"You're not going there tomorrow, Olive. You're never going over there."

She's flabbergasted.

95

"What do you mean I'm not going over there? I'm in the commercial. I have to be there. We have a rehearsal to do… don't we?"

"Olive, I hope you don't take this the wrong way, but you asked me to help you out with the harassing calls you were getting from Hal, and the fact that he threatened to blackmail you. Remember that?

"Well, I've put an entire plan into operation, and I think it's the only way we can ever get Hal out of your life. If you go to that production company, you'll be on his hook forever, and I can't imagine what he might ask for next time.

"Listen Olive, I want you to trust me on this one. Everything will become clear to you in the next month or so, and if it makes you feel any better, you've just earned your fee in full. Once I turn this tape over to the production company, you'll have seventy-five hundred dollars coming to you, and you don't have to do anything else to get it."

"How are they going to make the commercial without me? Hal wants me to call him tomorrow when I get to the production company, just to make sure everything is okay."

"Not to worry, kid. I've got that covered too."

7

The production company is calling. They don't know it yet, but the plan is proceeding perfectly.

"Mister Sharp, this is Nick at Volcano Productions. I'm afraid there's been some mix-up with the casting. A girl came in here and handed me your card, telling me to call you. She says she's supposed to star in the commercial. Is that correct?"

"That's right, Nick. Just to put your mind at ease, here's what I want you to do. Dial your sponsor's number on a cell phone and then give the phone to your star. She'll talk to him for a couple of minutes, and then she'll give the phone back to you. At that time, Mister Belsky, your sponsor, will personally let you know that she's approved for the job. That way, there's no responsibility on your part: you're just following orders."

"Okay Mister Sharp, but just between you and me, she wouldn't be my first choice for the part."

About a half hour later Nick calls me again.

"I don't believe it Mister Sharp. I did exactly what you told me to do. I called Mister Belsky's private line, and he answered. I know it was him because I recognized his voice. Then I told him that his star had arrived and he asked to speak to her. I handed her the phone, and she walked off to a corner of the room and started to sweet-talk him on the phone. I worked on a couple of porno films when I was first getting started in this business, but I never heard a conversation like that before. When she handed the phone back to me, it sounded like Mister Belsky was out of breath, but he definitely confirmed the fact that she was the female he wanted to star in this commercial."

"That's great, Nick. As they say in the business, break a leg."

It's now almost a month later and the newscasts are buzzing about a new sports car that's being introduced and how it will premier at Belsky's Beverly Hills Auto Mart. The promotion calls for the releasing of a television commercial that will coincide with the debut of the new car, a mock-up of which is now sitting in Belsky's showroom completely covered by a tarp. There is a cable coming down from the ceiling attached to the tarp. It looks like P.T. Belsky will be there to press a button and raise the tarp just as the commercial shows the real car is being driven into his showroom on 'premiere' night.

From what the newscasts show, the hour is rapidly approaching, and quite a crowd is outside his dealership, looking at the draped mock-up of the car, and waiting for the commercial to be shown on a group of large television screens that were installed for the onlookers.

Nick calls from Volcano Productions. "Hi Mister Sharp, I just wanted to make sure you received that fifteen-thousand-dollar check sent out for the star's appearance."

"Yes Nick, it arrived this afternoon. I guess you got paid for your company's work too?"

"Oh yeah. We never release the finished product until we receive the last payment for the assignment. I guess you know that tonight's the night. They're airing the commercial on all the major channels in this market, at five minutes to eight this evening. Those spots will also show on the large screens that the client has at his dealership."

"Yes Nick, I know. As soon as the spot has aired there'll be some sort of fanfare, and Mister Belsky will push a button that lifts up the tarp that's covering up the mock-up car, that will be pulled away and replaced by the real thing as your star drives it into the showroom.

"I hope he doesn't mind, Mister Sharp, but we had to make some slight changes to the beginning of the shooting script allow for some technical problems. The rest went along just as planned, including the slight difficulty we had while shooting some establishing shots outside at the dealership."

While we're on the phone, the first hour of prime time shows is finishing up, and at exactly seven fifty-five I see that Hal's commercial is starting to roll. The entire screen fills up with text informing the viewing public that what they're going to see is something they've never seen before.

"Nick, the commercial is going to start in a couple of seconds, so why don't you hang on the phone for the two minutes while it runs and let me watch it. I'm sure you'll want to view it too, to see the crowd reaction at the dealership."

I put the phone down on the table, sit back, and get ready to watch real creativity at work. I hope the kid sees this.

As planned, the commercial starts out with an announcer's voice-over that hawks the advantages of the new car, while the screen shows the first model slowly moving down the production line towards the last station, where it will be polished and driven out to the parking lot.

We hear how wonderful the car is, how great the mileage is, and a lot of other propaganda about safety, handling, reliability, yada yada. A worker gets in the car and drives from the last production point towards a large open door.

The next thing we see is a view from outside as he drives through the car factory's parking lot. We see the rear of the car as it starts to drive away. Strangely, the car seems to be tilting over on the driver's side. We are told that the car has been turned over to its spokesperson and she will be driving all the way to Beverly Hills. We see the female spokesperson's long hair waving in the wind as she rides away, and while some romantic music is being softly played in the background, we hear her sexy voice telling us how wonderful it is to be in this car.

Next shot is under some classical romance musical theme and we see the car off in the distance, heading toward us. It must be several miles away, but as it starts to get closer, we can see more clearly that it still does lean over, as if the tires on the driver's side of the car have been partially deflated, and the passenger side of the car is up higher off the ground.

As the car gets closer and we hear more sensual dialogue presumably from the driver, we see

101

that behind the wheel is a person that from far away closely resembles a huge Miss Piggy, of Muppet fame.

The next shot is from a camera car that is driving in front of the sports car, allowing the car to slowly approach and close the distance from about a quarter mile to only five or ten feet, and we see that stuffed into the driver's seat is none other than April May, our five-hundred pound client. I hear a yelp of laughter and a bark coming from the forward stateroom. Good. They're watching it too.

When the little car gets close behind the camera car, you can actually see the beads of perspiration streaming down April's face.

I hear roars of laughter coming out of my cell phone, as it sits on the coffee table next to me. It must be the crew at the production company, also watching this commercial.

The next scene is of April driving the car onto Hal's lot. Seeing her in that car looks a lot like ten pounds of something stuffed into a five-pound bag. The car is noticeably tilting over under her massive weight as it pulls into the showroom.

Another condition about Olive supposedly agreeing to be in the commercial is that on the afternoon when they shot this scene, that Hal wouldn't be there. He agreed, so this is the first time he's seeing his star.

She drives onto the showroom, and the drape is lifted up revealing the mock-up, which is quickly pulled out of the way to make way for the real thing. Once the car comes to a stop on the showroom floor, April does her best imitation of Meg Ryan's famous 'orgasm' scene from the movie *When Harry Met*

Sally. After her last moan, she releases the door latch, and the little door flies open with such force that it actually pops off one of its hinges and then limply swings back and forth a few times until coming to rest.

The next few seconds are a side-splitting attempt she makes to get out of the car. When April finally succeeds in getting her frame most of the way out from behind the wheel, she uses the steering wheel as support to lift herself the rest of the way out. At this point, we can clearly see that the steering wheel frame is being pushed down with such force that it actually bends, and we can hear the metal straining as the column is now in a permanently downward position, having been forced that way by April's weight.

Now almost out from behind the driver's seat, April loses her balance and reaches over toward the car, resting her hand on the outside rearview mirror, which promptly falls right off of the car, as if it was being held on by bubble gum. It makes a wonderful crash sound as it lands on the showroom floor and shatters. As April tries to steady herself, she reaches over and grabs onto the radio antenna, which gets pulled out of its socket by the force of her leaning on it. When it comes out of its molding, it takes a portion of the fender with it.

I'm having difficulty in controlling myself. The commercial ends and the station's news cameras then cut to show the expression on Hershel's face. Priceless. Now for the full-screen shot of the car, as April waddles out of the way.

And there it is, steering column bent out of shape, broken mirror on the floor, driver's door hanging crooked, hole in the outside of the door where the mirror had been bolted on, and partially damaged fender from which the radio antenna had been torn. The left rear tire also looks like it's slowly going flat. This poor little sub-compact sports vehicle looks like it just came through a war zone.

I haven't seen an expression like the one on Hershel's face since visiting a friend in Bucks County and encountering a deer caught in our headlights. The news cameras pick up the sound of an entire crowd outside the dealership roaring in laughter. There's also quite a bit of giggling coming from the forward stateroom. I pick up the phone to continue my conversation with Nick.

"Nick, you've outdone yourself. This has been the greatest commercial I've ever seen in my entire life. Would you please send me a DVD of it? I want to play it once in a while whenever I need a little cheering up."

"We already sent you one, Mister Sharp. You should be getting it tomorrow. Sorry about the changes we had to make at the beginning of the spot, but there was just no way that April could climb into that little car. After several tries we finally gave up and rolled the car back into the assembly area of the plant, where we used an engine-hoist to lift her up and then gently lower her into the driver's seat.

"Several mechanics at the factory said that the car would never make it to Los Angeles with that unbalanced load, so all we shot on the highway was the first few seconds. We trucked the car the rest of the way."

"How did you get her in and out of the car while you were trucking it?"

"Yeah, that was a problem… so we didn't. We left her sitting in it on back of the stake bed truck we hired. She rode in the little car, on the truck, all the way to Beverly Hills. But that wasn't the end. When you saw her bending the steering column to get out of the car, she really didn't make it all the way out. She fell back in, behind the wheel."

"A few seconds later she was almost standing outside the car."

"Yeah, but we had to bring in a forklift to get her out of it before we cut to the scene where it looked like she just got out of the car.

"I gotta tell you, Mister Sharp. I know it looked funny, but that girl April is one hell of a person. She knew how it looked and went along with it one hundred percent. She's a very nice person and by the end of the shoot, no one was laughing at her. In fact the whole crew gave her a round of applause when the last day wrapped and couldn't stop hugging her when we wrapped the shoot. She's a real trooper and we all shared the same feeling that it was a pleasure working with her."

As our conversation ends, I see the early news shows starting. There are several newscasters with camera trucks at the dealership and you can still hear laughter from the crowd. Hershel, being the showman that he is, regains his composure and saves the day with his clever remark.

"My wife always suspected me of having affairs with our spokes-models. I hope she trusts me from now on."

The only downside to this whole affair was the demeaning of April, because of her immense size.

105

We talked about it quite a bit when first discussing her doing the commercial, and she told me that people are going to laugh at her anyway, so she might as well make seventy-five hundred for accepting the laughter this time. I call to let her know that the entire production crew thinks the world of her... and so do I.

At one time she told me that she considered going on some special diet and even thought about having one of those surgeries, where they staple part of your stomach shut, but her boyfriend Joe talked her out of it. I guess as long as she's happy that's all that counts, but I keep remembering what a doctor friend of mine told me: you see a lot of old people, and you see a lot of fat people, but you rarely see any old fat people. I'd like to see her lose some weight, because it will mean a longer, healthier life for her.

Now all I have to do is finish with that apartment manager problem before the jerk tries to evict her.

Hershel Belsky wins again. The newspapers and television shows can't stop talking about Hershel's ad and even the network late night talk show hosts have made fun of it. Several organizations that represent fat people staged protests that didn't last too long, because after a while it became clear to most reasonable people that making fun of people who are morbidly obese just isn't satisfactory behavior. Some people have even suggested that Hershel should be rewarded for hiring a person with a weight problem like that.

I don't care what people say about Hershel or the commercial, as long as he doesn't call Olive any more. And it looks like the whole project worked. It's been several weeks since the commercial ran and Olive hasn't heard word one from him. In fact, the ad may have done him a great service. The last time I drove by his dealership, that exact same battered car was on the showroom floor, and they never even bothered to straighten out the steering wheel column or re-attach the damaged parts. From what I hear, the car has turned into a tourist attraction, with everyone wanting their picture taken with it. Hershel's salesmen are kept busy writing up orders, and the factory can't deliver the cars fast enough. Go figure.

They need my advice at the soundstage, so I'm on the way over there. Joe Caulfield is in his office waiting for me.

"Hi Peter, thanks for coming by so quickly. We're going to need your services again for a scene shooting tomorrow that takes place in a judge's chambers. By the way, how did your voice-over session go?"

"It went fine, thanks. Renaldo was nice enough to stay in the building to help me out. I paid him for his time, but I sure appreciate his hanging around the extra hour or so."

This gets a smile out of Joe.

"Well, it really wasn't too much of an inconvenience for him."

"Why not? It meant another two hours before he could get home and relax."

"Peter, Ren has an apartment upstairs of the soundstage. He's the resident manager of this place and runs it for the owners, who are also the investors in this picture we're shooting, the next two we have planned, and the new film courier service we're starting up. Thanks to Ren, we have exclusive use of this soundstage building, even when we're not shooting. He made that deal for us with the owners. And it was partly Ren's idea for the courier service too. He's a valuable employee around here, and a good worker too."

I'm glad to hear that Joe's business plans for the next couple of years are all in place and also happy to see that Ren is part of it all.

We go over some of the legal issues of tomorrow's scene until Joe is satisfied that the shot will work and also be fairly accurate with respect to actual legal procedures.

Back at the boat while doing the only kind of surfing I enjoy, which is completely out of the water and on the internet, I come across a website that is offering a DVD of a big budget movie that was recently released. This seems odd because I was under the impression that there was some 'window' of time that theater exhibitors demanded before a film was released on DVD. I don't blame them for that, because who wants to drive to an overpriced crowded theater with popcorn and spilled beverages on the floor, when you can sit at home and watch the same thing in the comfort of your own home?

I guess the window of time has expired because this particular movie is now available, and it's only twenty-five dollars, which includes shipping to me. I get my credit card out and click on the website's 'order' button. To my surprise, they don't accept credit cards. Instead they ask for the numbers off of my checking account, so that they can have a direct bank transfer of the funds from my bank to theirs.

This is okay with me, so I send a message to our office manager that I'm authorizing the charge, and provide the DVD sellers with the information they require to process the order. I've been an internet shopper for many years now, buying just about everything but shoes online, but this is the first time I've come across an e-merchant that doesn't accept credit cards. There must be a good reason for it, but as long as I get the merchandise that was ordered, whatever their reason is, it's okay with me.

The next day, I'm handed a U.S. Priority Mail package containing the DVD that I ordered. Suzi and Bernie made their morning run to our private mailbox place, and the movie was there, waiting to be picked up. Now that's what I call good service. There's no return address on the box, but it has a postmark indicating that it was mailed last night from a post office in San Pedro, California, which is about thirty miles down the coast, near the Port of Los Angeles.

There's no time like the present to see a good movie, so I put the DVD into my player and sit back to watch it on our fifty-two-inch flat-panel screen. The quality is excellent and I'm totally satisfied with the product, but I'm not one to fool around much with the 'menu' button or watch those other options that they put on DVD's. Just out of curiosity, I press the 'menu' button to see what I'm missing. Quite often when they release a movie on DVD they add comments from the director and stars, some out-takes, maybe an optional ending they shot, and some other bells and whistles. Not this time. This DVD was the movie, period. No extra bells and whistles. That works for me. I now have the movie in my collection, and that's all I was really expecting.

Strolling down the dock, I bump into Tony, who tells me that some assistant from the soundstage called and said that Joe wants to meet with him tonight. This probably means I'll be going over there tomorrow to try and get Tony's job back for him. Amazingly, he hasn't been fired in a while, and he's certainly due. I just hope there's no gunfire during their meeting tonight.

And speaking of shots on the soundstage, I recently got shot down there by a pretty young starlet who told me that I reminded her of 'her dad,' because he has a boat too. Not willing to let it go at that, I've had further conversations with her, and surprise of surprises, I have a dinner date tonight. Not with the pretty young starlet, but with her divorced mother, who hopefully still has an affinity for boats. I haven't the slightest idea of what she looks like, but her daughter says that she's attractive, and seeing what type of genes are in that family, I've got to take a shot at this.

We're supposed to meet at Pollo Meshuga. I picked the place because it worked so well for my recent dinner with Myra, I want to see if the restaurant can work its charms again.

One interesting thing about the place is the numerous television sets hung from the ceiling throughout the dining room. Tonight I'm not going to be watching them, because a woman just walked in the front door who I am now praying is my date. I prefer redheads, but I'll make an exception for her, because she's a grown-up version of the blonde starlet who set us up. She stops at the reservation desk and is directed towards my table. I can tell that her body is in pretty good shape because she's wearing a pair of tight jeans, and she's walking in my direction. She smiles when she sees me, sticks out her hand as a greeting, and says "Hello Peter, I'm Evelyn, your date." Yes! There is a God.

I walked over to the restaurant, so there's no hesitation in ordering another round of Patrón margaritas when she sits down. I'm already one up on her. After about half a drink and fifteen minutes, the conversation is going on like we've known each other for years. We talk about everything from movies, to the law, to boats, and anything else that comes up.

She already knows that I'm a lawyer who lives on a boat, and must have done some checking up, because she also is aware of the fact that I had been married to the current District Attorney of our County.

This restaurant was a favorite place for my ex-wife and I to frequent and I was really hoping to not have her name come up here, because it makes me feel like Myra is haunting the place while I'm here with someone else. I change the subject as quickly as possible, so that no thought of Myra will cloud my already foggy brain, when my date points out to me that my ex-wife is now in the room.

If you went to Las Vegas, I'm sure you could get odds of at least ten thousand to one that Myra wouldn't show up here, in this restaurant, tonight, while I'm here on a date with another woman. I carefully look around the room, when my date points something out to me. "No, silly, I don't mean she's here in the restaurant... she's up there, on the television screen."

I look up and sure enough, there she is, looking as good as ever. I signal the bartender to turn the volume up, and we hear the newscaster standing next to her make the introduction: "I'm standing here in front of the Criminal Courts Building in downtown Los Angeles, with Myra Scot, the District Attorney. Miss Scot, would you please tell our viewers about the arrest?" Myra takes the microphone from the newscaster's hand, and as usual, takes over the newscast.

"Our office has made an arrest this evening. We are charging a man with the murder of a film executive. Later this week, we will be going to the grand jury to get an indictment on this case."

The newscaster has a question. "Miss Scot, if you've already made the arrest, why are you going for an indictment? Isn't the regular procedure for you to just charge the defendant and set the matter for a preliminary hearing?"

Myra has an answer, but it's definitely not the one that I want to hear.

"Yes, that would be the ordinary procedure, but in this case the suspect is a twenty-year veteran of the police department, and is also a detective, so we're treating this matter in a way consistent with the reasons that the grand jury was formed... to investigate allegations of misconduct and crime of persons in official positions."

"Miss District Attorney, if you won't reveal the name of the defendant, can you at least tell us something about the victim, and the crime?"

"Yes, I can. I've been informed there have already been notifications made to the family, so I can tell you that the victim was a film producer named Joseph Caulfield, who was in the process of shooting a motion picture at a studio in Venice, California."

8

I knew it. Everyone knew it. It was just a matter of time before Tony shot Joe Caulfield. Not only was Tony a loose cannon, he was a loose cannon who carried a cannon, and didn't care for people of color. I don't know if he's retained a lawyer yet, but I sure hope he does, because this is not a case I feel like getting involved with. I know too much about the relationship between the suspect and the victim, and somewhere in the pit of my stomach I think that Tony actually did it. He may not be guilty of murder in the first degree, but unless it was self-defense, he's surely looking at some degree of manslaughter – but that's only if the D.A.'s office is willing to deal.

Knowing Myra, she'll probably not want to plead this case out for anything less than murder one if I'm the defense attorney, for fear of making it look like she's doing a favor for her ex-husband. Boy, if the public only knew how much that's not possible.

Needless to say, this has put a slight damper on my first date experience. Evelyn obviously had heard the news about conflicts between Tony and Joe from her daughter. "Well, at least he hasn't called you to represent him."

"To be quite honest, I've had my telephone turned off since you walked into this place, and I'm afraid to turn it back on, because it might mean our evening will end before it should."

I don't know how such a nice statement ever came out of my mouth. As I hear it, I'm saying to myself 'what wimp is saying this?' It seems to have worked, because there's a slight blush on her cheeks as she reaches forward and takes my hand.

"You'd better turn your phone on. We can always get together again, but your friend Tony may have only one phone call coming to him."

She's right. Grudgingly, I turn on the phone, and as soon as the signal strength comes up to par, I see that there are several voice messages waiting for me. When checking them out, there are no surprises. The first one is from Tony, and subsequent ones are from Suzi and Myra. They all give me the same information: like it or not, I have a new client.

Having a cop for a client has its advantages. First, you get treated with respect by other cops, because now you're on their side, representing one of them. Second, you don't have to worry about your client blabbing anything that can be used against him.

After Evelyn leaves the restaurant I call Myra at home.

"You got my call, huh?"

"Yeah, but you could have saved me the dime by adding another sentence to your on-camera interview. All you had to do was say 'Peter, get your ass down to central booking, someone wants to see you.' That would have saved some time, too."

"I actually considered doing that, but I know that you don't take orders from me anymore, so I called Suzi instead. Let her tell you what to do, because God knows you need direction."

"If he's at County Jail, I'm on the way down there. Would you please do me a favor and call the kid to let her know I'll be late tonight?"

"No need, she already knows. And your client is not at County Jail, he's in the Venice Police Station."

"Aha, that must mean you haven't got as good a case as you thought you did."

"Wrong again, Peter. I had other reasons to put him there tonight. I suppose you'll be in court tomorrow with a bail motion?"

"I will be if you intend to charge him."

"See you in court tomorrow Peter."

The jailer at Los Angeles Police's Venice Division knows me. I've been to his establishment many times as a lawyer and once as a tenant. I see that Tony is being treated nicely, because he's not in a cell. Instead, he's sitting at a table, playing cards with the jailer.

As I figured, he didn't make any statements to anyone, and they knew better than to ask him any questions.

"Okay Tony, let's hear it. From the time that someone called you on your boat."

"As I told you, some production assistant whose voice I didn't recognize called me. Joe and I were having some differences about tomorrow's scenes, so I figured he had someone call me to come in for a meeting. The PA told me that they would probably wrap the day's shoot between six and seven, so I should drop by at eight. I was told that the back door to the stage would be left ajar for me, but I was supposed to make sure that I locked it from the inside after I came in.

"I got there at seven fifty-five, came in the back door, locked it after I came in, and then went to

Joe's office. He wasn't there, so I sat down and waited for him. I figured he was in the head or something. After about ten or fifteen minutes, he didn't show up, so I started walking around the building, calling out his name.

"I checked all the rooms except for the soundstage. When I went back there, it was still dark, so I flipped on the house lights. Then I saw him. He'd been drilled right through the middle. I must have passed him by when I walked through the dark stage. I didn't touch him, or anything else. I used my cell phone to call the uniforms. When they arrived, they confirmed what I already knew: he was shot in the chest. The bullet went clear through him and flattened itself out on the concrete wall of the soundstage, after it penetrated the soundproofing.

"As a routine matter, they asked if I was armed, and I opened my coat to let them see my S & W 500. They took it out of my holster and sniffed it. They realized that it had been fired, and they were right, because I was out at the range today. That's where I was coming from when you saw me on the dock.

"When they checked my weapon, they saw one expended round. That's when they gave me my rights and brought me here. I don't know how that empty casing got there, and I swear to you, I didn't shoot Joe."

"They've got a long way to go before they have an airtight case against you, so relax. I talked to the D.A. and she's meeting me in court tomorrow, where we'll be fighting over your bail. At least she gave you a break by sending you here instead of to County Jail. I'll see you in court tomorrow."

The next morning Myra is in rare form. Not only does she look good, but she sounds good too. The usual procedure takes place. After the bailiff announces that we should remain seated and come to order, he says the judge's name, the man with the robe walks in from his private entry, steps up to the bench, sits down, and the clerk calls the first case... Tony's. The judge starts.

"Good morning counsel. I see that we're honored by the attendance of the District Attorney herself. Is that because you're here, Mister Sharp?"

"I've given up trying to imagine what type of food coaxes her out of the cage Your Honor, so it must be for the purpose of starting one of her office's weakest cases."

Myra looks at me for a few seconds until she runs out of daggers. The judge continues.

"Okay, boys and girls, we've got an arraignment to do here now. I see that the Defendant is present in court, and I know who the players are, but why don't you say your names anyway, just for the record?"

We comply with his request, and he goes to the next phase.

"We have a charge of Penal Code Section 187 being made by the People today. Mister Sharp, am I correct in assuming that you and your client waive reading of the charges and enter a plea of not guilty?"

I let him know that he is correct. We all know what's next, so he doesn't disappoint us. "Miss Scot, I saw you on television last night and you hinted that you might be taking this case to the Grand Jury, am I to take it by your presence today that you've changed your mind?"

Myra confirms that he is correct, and that the case will be going through the normal channels, with a Preliminary Hearing being requested. The judge asks her the big question. "Do the People have any recommendation on bail?"

"Yes we do, Your Honor, we feel that bail should be denied and this defendant should be remanded to custody. The victim was shot by a large .50 caliber handgun, exactly like the one removed from the defendant's shoulder holster. We have witness statements to the effect that the defendant argued with the victim, and there was one empty shell casing in the defendant's recently fired weapon. The defendant was given a paraffin test to see if he fired a weapon shortly before the crime was committed. The results were positive. He failed."

The judge is surprised to hear about the gun and has a question.

"Did you say that it was a fifty caliber handgun that was used? I didn't know they made handguns that big. What are they good for, stopping runaway elephants?"

I better say something before this whole procedure turns into a circus. There are already quite a few reporters in the courtroom, and I don't want the public to get the feeling that Tony is a big game hunter who mistook the victim for black bear.

"Your Honor, the weapon that is being referred to is a popular new model manufactured by the Smith and Wesson Company, and quite a few police officers have decided to carry one just like it, in view of the heavily armed criminals who now are using military assault rifles.

"Furthermore, we would like to make the Court aware of the fact that it was the defendant who discovered the body and immediately called the police. There was a period of at least five minutes before the first squad car responded, Your Honor, and if my client had actually done the shooting, after having served more than twenty years on the police force, he certainly would not have been too much in shock to have realized that it was time to remove the empty casing from his weapon and quickly leave the scene.

"And as for the recent firing of his weapon and his results on the paraffin test, we also have witnesses to the fact that he was out on a shooting range shortly before this crime, firing his weapon.

"In view of the fact that there is no way the People can definitely link his gun to this crime, and also taking into consideration his calling the police, staying until they arrived, and fully cooperating in the investigation, we urge this court to recognize a man who has appeared here on many past occasions in the interest of supporting the law. We would ask that the defendant be released on his own recognizance."

This is not an uncommon request in cases like this. The People ask for a remand with no bail being set, and the defense asks for a no-bail release. The judge thinks about it for a minute before making his decision.

"I hear both of you, and ordinarily I'd tend to agree with the People, but I've seen this policeman testify in front of me plenty of times over the past fifteen years, and I'm of the opinion that he's to be trusted with bail. The remand is denied. As for the amount of bail, I also realize that this is a capital case, so I'm going to set the bail at one hundred thousand dollars. Check with my clerk for a Prelim date."

That being said, he bangs his gavel down with the usual "next case."

Tony looks at me with an expression probably most used by animals that are just about to be put asleep at the dog-pound. He knows that there's no way he can raise the money for bail, so he'll be spending quite a while in the County Jail, where the other prisoners don't exactly care for cops.

The bailiff walks over to us. "Counselor, you're free to go, and take your client with you. His bail has been posted."

Tony and I are both completely surprised by this. As Myra passes by on her way out of the courtroom, her comment gives me a hint as to how the bail was set. "I'll have to talk to that brat. She's starting to annoy me."

The Chinese restaurant around the corner is a very popular place for the police to congregate for lunch every day... and they do. On any given afternoon, the parking lot is full of black-and-white cars and motorcycles, and the inside is full of both dark blue and khaki uniforms. Because the kid's mother used to run the place, Suzi is a celebrity there, and is treated like a mascot by every cop in the place. They must like her, because she brings that huge Saint Bernard in there with her, and there's never been any complaint made to the Health Department about a dog being in a closed setting where food is served.

Over the past six years since her mother was killed in a car accident, Suzi is at the restaurant every day at lunchtime, and started working behind the cash register when she was only five years old, so she knows all the cops, and they know and adore her. She also does what she can to help divorced cops get slips in the Marina when their wives throw them out, and they decide to live on an old boat. I know what that feels like, because her late stepfather did the same for me.

Tony is one of the kid's cop lunch gang, so she felt honor-bound to bail him out. I can't complain. If she wants to use ten thousand of the firm's money for a bail premium, she must believe he's innocent – and if that's her feeling then he probably is, because no matter how bad things look for Tony now, she's usually right. I know it, and Myra knows it. That's probably what's bothering our District Attorney. Myra would never question her decision to file against someone if I was the one advising her against it, but she knows that the kid is usually dead-on with her little instincts.

I call April and try to console her. She isn't taking the loss of her boyfriend too well and I get the feeling that she feels awkward talking to the person who is representing the guy accused of killing Joe. Her apartment building manager must know that the victim they're talking about on television was April's boyfriend, so he's temporarily backed off of the eviction drive, probably to avoid getting involved with a high profile person who just lost her boyfriend to a murderer and was the star of one of the county's most popular car commercials. I tell her not to worry and that things will work out.

Tony and I are trying to figure out how to beat this case. "Tony, what about ballistics? Is there a way they can tie your gun into the shooting?"

"Remember counselor? I told you that ballistics was my weak suit. I've talked to a couple of old friends who told me that the bullet went right through Joe and flattened like a pancake when it hit the wall."

"All that proves is that you had an empty shell casing in your gun. That could be a coincidence. That's not enough to convict."

"Yeah, but I heard this morning that they found my fingerprints on that empty casing, just like on the other four bullets in the gun."

"So what? It was your gun. I'd be more surprised to find a bullet in there that didn't have your fingerprints on it."

"Nice try counselor, but every cop you talk to will tell you that you never leave empty casings in your weapon after firing it. Either you carry a fully loaded weapon or you don't carry one at all. If they've got an empty casing, they'll believe that it was used to shoot Joe. And you know what? He's the first black guy I was ever on the verge of becoming friendly with. He was tough to work with, but he knew what he was doing, and I now realize that I was wrong almost every time we argued. Do you think they'll stop production of the movie?"

"No. If I'm right about those sharks that make movies nowadays, they'll probably use Joe's death to some advantage for publicizing the picture when it's released."

I was right. Back at the soundstage production is going on as usual. Everyone is sorry that Joe was killed, but they also value their high paying jobs. I've got an appointment with the person taking Joe's place. Ren called letting me know that he wants to talk about Tony.

Joe's replacement is a man named Will Sargent. He welcomes me into his office.

"Mister Sharp, thanks for coming in. Can I call you Peter? Good. I just want you to know that we intend to finish this production, but there's one more scene that requires Tony to be in it, and I want to know what your thoughts are on that."

"That's an easy one, Will. Tony is innocent and I intend to prove it. There's no way he would have shot Joe, left an empty bullet in his gun, and then called the police to report the crime. He's being framed plain and simple, and I see no reason why you shouldn't let him do that last scene he's supposed to be in for two main reasons. First, if you don't let him continue, you'll have to re-shoot every scene in the movie that he appeared in and that will cost time and money. Second, if he's in the film, you'll have double the impact for advertising when the picture is released. If he's convicted, the people will flock to see a murderer in the picture. If he's acquitted, he can do the talk show circuit for you. It's a win-win for your production company."

"You've got some nice points there, Peter, but I've got one more consideration."

"What would that be, Will?"

"The rest of the cast and crew. If they refuse to work with him, then there's nothing I can do."

"Okay Will, I'll talk to them. But if I can get them to agree to work with Tony, then do we have a deal? Tony can continue in the picture?"

We shake on it and I go onto the soundstage to campaign for my client.

It was a lot easier than I thought it would be. I've heard stories about film crews who work long, hard hours together and consider themselves like family, but never actually saw it happen… until now.

It was almost unanimous. They worked with Tony, saw him struggle with the acting process, helped him out in any way they could, and there seems to have been some bond formed between them and him, but you'd probably never get him to admit it.

I spent a good deal of time making my presentation to them about how I believed he was innocent, and gave all the arguments against guilt and the holes in the prosecution's case. It wasn't until after it was all over and everyone agreed that Tony should come back to finish the picture that I realized where my presentation took place: the set, which is decorated to look exactly like a courtroom. I now realize that what I was doing was a rehearsal of my summation to the jury. I've heard of mock trials before where a trial and summation is practiced, but those things are supposed to cost many thousands of dollars. Thanks to the Venice Soundstage, I just got one for free. One more benefit was the very obvious wink that I got from one young starlet. I imagine she feels like a new step-dad is in the wings. The most amazing thing about my presentation is that it was mostly acting, because I still have my doubts about Tony's innocence.

Back at the boat I call Tony and leave a message on his answering machine that he'd better be ready to go back to work, because the whole film company is expecting him back on the stage to finish his last scene. I also add a brief explanation about my speaking to everyone in the company, and that it was a unanimous decision on their part. Next time I see Ren on the stage, I'll have to thank him. My job was so easy there, I'm sure he must have paved the way for my summation by telling everyone how strongly he believed in Tony's innocence.

The phone rings. It's Stuart calling. He sounds cryptic today, like he's afraid someone's listening in.

"Peter, can we get together some time soon?"

"Sure Stu, what's on your mind?"

"I'd rather tell you when I see you."

"C'mon Stuart, at least give me a hint."

"Okay. You know that thing I'm doing from the left coast to the right coast? You know, that unmentionable new business deal I've recently started?"

He must be talking about his cross-country gambling scheme, where he bets against himself on home teams playing baseball. For some reason, he's become paranoid about it. I get the hint that he doesn't even want to use the word 'bet' or 'gambling' on the phone, so I might as well play along with him.

"Stuart, I think I know exactly what you're talking about, but if you only want to get together with me to try and get me involved in participating, I'm really not interested."

"No, Pete, it's not that. It's that I'm uh, well, I'm worried about one aspect of it. You know, it involves activities in more than one state, and I'm concerned about Federal law. Can you please look into it for me? I'd feel a lot better knowing that I'm only breaking local misdemeanor rules, if anything at all."

I assure Stuart that I'll look into it, and also mention the new DVD I received. It features one of his favorite stars, so he asks if he can borrow it.

There's a possibility I can kill three birds with one stone this afternoon. I can stop by the Federal Building in West Los Angeles to discuss a hypothetical case with an FBI Agent that I know there. Then I can drive over to Stuart's warehouse in Van Nuys to put his mind at ease, and also give him that DVD to watch.

FBI Special Agent Snell's office says that he's in and can give me a few minutes of his time, so I'm on the way there. Last year I helped him take the credit for breaking up a bank robbery gang, and more recently, a case I was handling enabled him to get the goods on a Mafia kingpin he'd been after for. Never in a million years would he ever say thank you or give me credit for helping him, but he does at least make himself available to me on occasion if I have a question about the Federal law.

There's no smile, and no handshake offered when I'm shown into his office. The most I can ever expect from him is that he remembers my name.

"Hello, Sharp. What do you want today?"

"Glad I caught you in a good mood. I'd like to run a hypothetical case by you, just to see if there are any Federal laws being broken."

Silence. He doesn't respond. He just sits there and stares at me. Typical prosecutor attitude, and I should be used to it by now. The sun is really shining today, and I didn't want to leave that DVD in the car, so I've had it in my hand for a while, and decide to put it down on Snell's desk, freeing up my hands. I always like to have free hands while I'm talking.

I start to explain about the 'what if' of a guy who makes bets with bookies on different coasts, and vaguely mention some of the details about what Stuart is now doing. This doesn't seem to interest him too much, so I'm feeling good already. Instead of asking me questions, Snell picks up the DVD off of his desk, and starts flipping it around between both of his hands.

The whole story about my hypothetical case is finished and Snell still looks bored. His answer is typical.

"There are people all over this country making bets with bookies every minute of the day. I guess that if we really looked at each case, we could find some law they're breaking... using the phone lines, using the U.S. Mail, I don't know, but I'm sure we could find something. But to tell you the truth, we don't have the time for that small stuff. It's just not that high on our priority list until someone other than a degenerate gambler complains that he's been seriously injured as the result of a criminal conspiracy.

"What's this, a porno movie you brought for me to watch?"

I reach across the desk to retrieve it, but he pulls back and opens the case.

"No Snell, sorry to disappoint you, but unless you think that Warner Brothers is now making porno, that DVD isn't for you. I didn't want to leave it in a hot car out in the parking lot. I'm bringing it to a client who wants to borrow it and let his relatives' kids watch it. But, if you're really interested in porno, there's a video store on Lincoln, around the corner from the Marina, where I understand they've got a great selection. Why don't I get you a gift certificate from them, and then you can use it over there.

"Now, can I please have my DVD back? I'd like to get on the freeway before the traffic gets too heavy."

"I'm afraid not, Sharp. In fact, I don't even know if you'll be on the freeway this afternoon. You're not going anywhere."

"What are you talking about?"

"Peter Sharp, you are in possession of a counterfeit DVD, and in violation of Title 17, United States Code Sections 501 and 506."

9

I had a feeling this particular movie was being released on DVD a little earlier than it should be, but I never believed that they'd be openly selling counterfeits on the internet. Maybe that's why they don't take credit cards and insist on only direct bank transfers of funds.

Snell is no different than my ex-wife or any other prosecutor in the world. Their first tactic is to totally disarm you mentally with a threat of prosecution. Their next move is to capitalize on your being immobilized with fear and willing to tell them anything they want to know, incriminating everyone including yourself. I've seen the game played plenty of times, but don't particularly feel like playing it today. I hold my hands out across the desk.

"Okay officer, you caught me. I'm guilty. Put the cuffs on my wrists and take me downtown to the Federal slammer."

No reaction from Snell. He just sits there glaring at me. Since he doesn't take me up on my offer of surrender, I might as well sit down again and start playing my own game.

"You really think I came up here to waste your time with some cross-country betting scheme? I was wondering how long it would take you to actually discover a violation of Federal law if it was put on your desk, right under your nose. The answer is exactly thirteen minutes. That's not bad, considering it was handed to you on a silver platter, and you actually played with it for over three of those thirteen minutes before finding out what you had in your hands.

"Now, do you want to continue playing some stupid cops-and-robber game with me, or are you interested in getting after some real bad guys. I haven't seen you on the front pages recently, so since I'm probably your best press agent, I thought I'd stop by and see if we can get the public interested in you again. Maybe we can revive this sagging career of yours. You know, I wouldn't be surprised if some of this big money these guys rake in is being used to finance terrorism."

Ah, the 'T' word. This gets a rise out of him, and out of the other two statues standing in his office. If not for the use of that word, you wouldn't know they were alive.

"All right Peter, enough. You've got my attention. Talk to me. Where did you get this DVD, and what are your plans. But before we start, I just want to know one thing. Is anyone involved in this stuff a client of yours?"

The big breakthrough is the fact that he used my first name. I always like to hear that, because it's a 'tell.' Whenever someone tries to get informal, it usually means that they want something from you. He asked a question, so he's entitled to an answer.

"No, I'm not representing anyone involved in this stuff. I'm here today as an innocent citizen who was taken in by some crooks. I'm writing a website address down on this piece of paper, and if that computer next to your desk is hooked up to the internet, I'd like you to go to this website and see what they're offering."

I slide the piece of paper across the desk to him. He hands it to one of his assistants, who promptly pulls up a chair, logs on, and goes to the website. Once the site appears on their screen, Snell nods at the other assistant, who leaves the room.

"I know what you're doing. You just told your man to find out who owns that URL. I already did that. It's an offshore company. And I can save you guys some money, too. You don't have to waste your time ordering one of those DVD's just to follow the money, because they don't leave a paper trail.

"If you go further into their website, you'll see that they don't accept credit cards. That would be too easy to trace because it would require their having filled out a complete application form to get a merchant approval number. These guys are smarter than that. Instead of credit cards, they ask for your bank checking info and have a wire transfer of the funds directly from your account to theirs. I'm sure that the money doesn't sit in that first account too long, because it probably gets ping-ponged from account to account, from country to country, while they siphon off funds in each transfer."

I amaze myself at this instant scenario creation, but these thoughts really had entered my mind when I first placed my order. Snell is deep in thought. I decide to help him out a little more.

"Funny thing, but when I ordered this, it was delivered the very next day... by U.S. Priority Mail. Of course there was no return address, but the postmark did show that it was mailed in San Pedro... about thirty miles away from where we are now sitting.

"That means we aren't dealing with some guys in a cave somewhere out in Afghanistan. They've got roots right here in this town. And that means you should be able to find them. With my help, of course.

"I know that you guys are certain that you can find these crooks without my help, but sooner or later you're going to need a private citizen who'll cooperate and front for you, and since I'm already on their customer list, I'm a prime candidate. They've got my email address, and I'm already starting to get announcements from them about upcoming releases. Now, if you will please authorize my reimbursement for this DVD and another couple that I will order, we'll have a chance to see if they're all dropped in the same mailbox."

"I can't authorize small sums like this, but keep track of your expenses and I'll see that you get reimbursed when the case is over. And please..."

"Yeah, I know. As soon as the mail is delivered to my P.O. box, I'll put on the gloves, bag it, and let you know to send someone over to get it. By the way, I'll be needing this one for a few days."

I reach across the desk and pick up my DVD. The case is empty. His assistant probably took it while we were looking at his computer screen. They obviously wanted to dust it for prints. Snell pushes a button on his desk and the assistant comes into his office with the disc in his hand. Snell looks up at him.

"Anything?"

"Yes sir, there were 'identifiables' from at least three different people."

"Well, one of them is sitting here at the desk. Give him the disc and let me know if you get any hits on the other two."

I put the disc in its case and leave. Once again, the game is afoot.

Stuart is pleased to hear that he's in no danger of imminent arrest, and he's also glad for the loan of the DVD. I turn down his offer for a late lunch because I know that I've got two new messes to take care of - Tony's and Snell's. I started the ball rolling with Snell, so now I'll have to do some investigation. I call the office and leave word on the kid's answering machine that we've got a new mystery to solve. She loves stuff like that, so I'll bet that by the time I get back to the boat she'll already be heavily involved in solving the case.

I want to help out a little too, so I call Jack Bibberman and give him a new assignment. I'd like him to find more out about the Volcano Production Company. Someone there wanted Joe Caulfield dead and took the opportunity to frame Tony for it. This doesn't look like it was a crime of passion, so that leaves only one other alternative: money. Love and money are the two main driving forces for most murders.

So far we already have two of the three requirements that Myra will be wanting to prove up: Means was no problem because all it took was one shot. Opportunity was there because Joe was alone on the soundstage after hours. That leaves motive as the problem. Why would anyone want him dead? I don't think it was because he was dating a morbidly obese white girl, so there must be some other answer.

My cell phone was switched off while I was in Snell's FBI office and I forgot to turn it back on when I was at Stuart's place. Turning it on now, there's a message waiting for me, and I'm happy to see that it's someone I was hoping would call. Evelyn. I return her call and apologize for not getting back to her sooner. She wants to get together, so we make plans to try Pollo Meshuga again. Maybe this time Myra will do me a favor and stay off of the television screens during our date.

Walking down our dock I see that Tony is having a meeting on his boat. Every guy he's talking to has a cop moustache and is wearing polyester, so it looks like he's busy working on his own case. That's good, because I can use all the help he can give me.

After a shower and shave, I've got about ten minutes to walk over to the corner restaurant to meet Evelyn. As I pass by his boat, Tony motions for me to come aboard.

"Hi Tony, I saw you had a police convention here earlier today. Any results?"

"Not yet, but there will be, I'm sure of it. My guys and I have been investigating cases like this for enough years to know a frame when we see it. The way we have it figured, there was some reason why Joe had to be whacked, and when I came along they saw a convenient patsy. They needed someone from the outside to do it so that after the arrest they could still keep going with the film. That means whoever's behind it has a vested interest in the film being completed.

"They only brought two new people in on the production after they started, and we guess that you weren't a good enough candidate for framing, so they waited until you sent them a better one.

"When I came along, they thought that all their prayers had been answered. I fit all the requirements: a cop suspended for shooting black people, a reputation as a racist, and constant conflicts with the black victim. It couldn't have been better if they wrote it like that. I was perfect, and it only took them long enough to figure how to build the frame."

"That sounds good Sarge, but do you have any suspects yet?"

"Yeah, as a matter of fact we do."

"Who? Any names I might recognize?"

"Sorry counselor, but this is an ongoing investigation so I can't discuss it with you."

"Are you kidding? What do you mean you can't discuss it with me? I'm your attorney. I'm the guy who fought to get you back on the picture. I'm the guy who'll be arguing for your acquittal at the trial. You have to tell me what you've got."

"Listen here Mister Lawyer, there isn't going to be a trial. I appreciate the fact that you're on my side and fought to get me back on the picture, but the real reason I wanted to return to the stage was not to be an actor. I had to get back with the production company so I could be on the inside. It was all for the investigation. Right now, I'm the most visible undercover cop in town. I know that you want to win the case, but do yourself a favor. Whoever was behind the murder of Joe Caulfield won't hesitate to kill anyone else who gets in the way.

"I'm no threat to them now, because they think the murder charge has already taken me out of the game, but you're another story. If you get too close to finding a skeleton in the closet, they won't hesitate to whack you. And I don't want to see that happen, because they'll probably try to frame me for your death too."

"So what you're telling me here is that you want me to mind my own business and stay out of investigating your case, because you're afraid of getting framed for another murder?"

"That's about the size of it. Besides, you've got a nice little kid on that boat of yours, and I think you should stick around for a while and watch her grow up."

Well what do you know? I finally found a soft spot. He wants me to think that it's another frame-up that worries him, but he really wants the kid to have a father figure around. Either way, it looks like he doesn't give a darn about me. It's himself or the kid that he's concerned with. That's okay, I'll take any small amount of concern.

Looking at my phony Rolex, a gift last year from Stuart, I see that spending the extra time with Tony has made me perilously close to being late for my dinner date with Evelyn, so I rush off the dock towards the restaurant.

Pollo Meshuga doesn't offer valet parking, but they do have a nice parking lot with a path leading up to it from our anchorage. On the way to the restaurant I see the Asian Boys walking the other way. I guess they're on their way to one of the boats to do some work.

It's just starting to get dark and I see a beautiful new Japanese top-of-the-line SUV pulling in to park. This thing looks brand new and must cost as much as my Hummer, because I've seen them advertised on television with a price 'as low as' fifty-three thousand. This one looks fully loaded, so with all the accessories and sales tax, it's probably well over sixty grand. Even more attractive than the vehicle is the driver. It's Evelyn. I pause for a second to give her a chance to walk into the restaurant. It would be bad form for me to accost her in the parking lot. It's dark in the corner where she parked, and I wouldn't want to give her the idea that I'm a stalker.

I catch up to her at the reservation desk, and after a polite peck on the cheek for a greeting, she holds my hand as we follow the seating guy to our table, which is by a window that overlooks that part of the Marina where my boat is docked. Sitting there with that view in front of us naturally leads the conversation to boating. She starts the questioning.

"How do you like living on a boat? My daughter mentioned you said you had one out here somewhere."

I point to the most recognizable thing near my boat, which is George Clooney's four-story high vessel. "You see that mega-yacht down the basin over there? Well it's not mine, but mine is just a few boats away from it. And to answer your question, I like it a lot. It's quiet and peaceful, and like being in a summer home at the beach.

"Your daughter mentioned that her father used to like boats. What did he do, change his mind?"

"No, he died."

I did it again. One of these days they're going to find a cure for foot-in-mouth disease, and I'm going to be the first one in line at the pharmacy. I use my best courtroom training to try and recover from this goof.

"Oh, I'm sorry. I didn't know. Well, that makes you the prettiest widow in this restaurant."

Nice try you jerk, but it didn't work. Right after the other cure, someone will write a book entitled 'things I should've said,' and after I'm through at the pharmacy, I'll be the first one in line at the bookstore.

"Actually, I'm not a widow. We were divorced several years before his accident, and he was already involved with another woman. For once, his timing was right, and he died before he had a chance to marry her or change his will, so my daughter and I came out of it quite well. It was really over for the last couple of years while we were married, so there wasn't too much grieving involved. I wasn't happy to see him dead, but I wasn't too happy to see him alive with that bimbo either. I hope you won't think poorly of me for those feelings, but that's the way it was. No sugarcoating, just the truth."

That answers another question. Now I know how she can afford that new SUV.

"How's your daughter taking it? Does she miss him?"

"At first she was devastated when he died, but after a while it became obvious that he was so involved with his new girlfriend that he just couldn't spend the time to pay attention to his own daughter. Maybe it's because the new love of his life was only a little older than his own daughter."

"If you don't mind my asking, how did he die?"

"Oh that's okay, it's a matter of public record. He was taking a helicopter from the airport to the top of his office building, and the ship's door was a defective. He fell out. I don't know what a door like that is, but my lawyers got the other side to admit to the fact that it was defective, and they paid for their mistake. So, along with the insurance policies and sale of the boat and other some other properties we owned, I can now afford to hang around here and meet you for lunch or dinner as often as you want. How does that sound?"

Fortunately, I don't have to answer because the waiter stopped by to deliver another round of Patrón margaritas. This is starting to look too good to be true. A beautiful and intelligent female with plenty of money, and she seems attracted to me. The last time I got lucky like this I got framed for murder. I'll ask Stuart to check with his bookies to see what the odds of the same thing happening to me twice in a twelve month period are. I was hoping that the drinks being delivered would create a pause that would give me an opportunity to change the subject completely, but I was wrong. She pushes ahead with the questioning.

"Peter, have you ever considered getting married again, or did the District Attorney turn you off of that institution?"

"Yes, I've thought about it, but that was before I had a kid."

This takes her aback. "You had a child after your divorce?"

I can see that she's curious about this, so seeing as it's a relaxing dinner and we're each imbibing a little, I take my and time and tell her the whole story, including my divorce, being thrown out of the house into the old boat in the backyard, The Lahaina Yacht Club, moving to the Marina, working for Mel, the old boat burning up, Melvin dying and leaving Suzi in my care, the Saint Bernard, how the firm works and just about everything else I can think of. After a while, I realize that I've been talking non-stop for the better part of the last hour… and through two more drinks.

"I'm sorry Evelyn, but you asked for it. Now you've got it. My entire life story."

Not only did she sit there and listen the whole time, she actually looked interested in what I was saying. Of course her next move was to ask to see the boat and meet Suzi, but I don't think she's ready for that yet, so I stall.

"C'mon, Peter. You've already met my daughter. I should have the same privilege."

"Your right beautiful, but the main difference here is that mine is a little genius princess who needs to be properly prepared, because if I don't do a good job of getting her ready to meet you, when you leave the boat, she'll flash a 'thumbs-down' sign at me, and then I may not be given permission to ever see you again."

"Well, handsome, I can see that you know how to handle a big girl, but you've got a lot to learn about handling a little one."

She may have a point there, but if she only knew how I screwed up my marriage to Myra, she might not have the same opinion of my ability to handle a big girl either.

The evening comes to a pleasant end without my being cornered into extending an invitation to the boat. I'll have to talk to the kid first, because every time she thinks I'm in danger of getting involved with any woman other than Myra, they put their heads together to let me know why it can never work out. First there was Patty, who they accused of being

141

a lesbian. Then there was Beverly Luskin, who tried to get me convicted of murder. The bad thing about Suzi and Myra is that they're rarely wrong.

I think I'll leave them out of the loop this time. I'd rather not give them a crack at Evelyn. I don't know too much about her, but I feel pretty sure that neither she nor her daughter were involved in any murder plots.

I walk her to the car, get my kiss goodnight, and stagger back to the boat. I don't understand it. She drank as much as I did, but I can hardly see where I'm walking and she looks completely unaffected.

Now back on board, I see some messages waiting for me. Olive wants me to know that she hasn't heard from Hal recently, so my plans worked. She's using the money she earned for not appearing in the commercial on her honeymoon with Vinnie.

Stuart called to thank me for letting him borrow that DVD, but complained that something must be wrong with it, because he couldn't access the Menu feature by using his player's remote control.

Tony called to make sure I wasn't getting in his way in the murder investigation, and Special Agent Snell wants me to buy some more DVDs off of that website.

I haven't heard from April for a while, so I won't bother her with a phone call. It looks like she's not being bothered by her apartment manager, and I want to give her some time to grieve over the loss of her boyfriend.

It's late in the evening, but I know that the counterfeit DVD website works around the clock, so I go to their website and order two more titles. Snell and his group will no doubt be watching them all the way through, so I make a special effort to select the most boring 'chick flicks' in their catalog. I also check with the local video store that's open all night to verify that these particular titles won't be available on video or DVD for another couple of months. This lets me know for sure that I'm ordering pirated movies. I then make a note to tell the guy at the private mailbox place to not touch those boxes, because they're going to be fingerprinted. He looks like he's been in the system before, so I'm sure he'll take my advice and keep his hands off of my mail. Before turning in, I leave two plastic evidence bags out for the kid, with a note telling her to bag the DVD's that come in and then call Snell's office so a messenger can be sent to pick them up. I'm amazed that I can think of all these things so clearly. It must have been the combination of Evelyn and the Patrón margaritas that increased my brain's powers. I'll have to try this experiment again soon.

I refuse to have an alarm clock anywhere near my sleeping quarters, and always make sure to turn off the landline and cell phone ringers before turning in. I'm not a doctor on call for emergency surgery, so there's no situation I can think of that's important enough to wake me up before I'm good and ready. The kid and dog both know where I am if a need should arise, and everyone else in the world can wait until I wake up the next morning.

Hershel Belsky didn't want to wait. When I turn on my cell phone this morning, I see that he called six times while I was sleeping. There are also a bunch of messages on my machine, so I guess he's trying every way he can to reach me.

One of the messages on my voice mail is from Nick at Volcano Productions. He also wanted to let me know that Hershel was desperately trying to reach me.

I quickly go through all of my messages and erase the ones from Hershel. An email comes in from him. I'm starting to get the idea that he really wants to talk to me, so I might as well call.

Beverly Hills is one of the most land-locked areas in the Los Angeles area. There's no freeway going there, so you have to suffer the traffic and exorbitant parking fees, which are doubled for me, because the parking guys charge my Hummer for two spots. The last time I visited a friend's office in Beverly Hills, it cost me over fifteen bucks to drive there and have him buy me a fourteen-dollar lunch. In addition to hating traffic, going to Beverly Hills just doesn't make economical sense to me, so whatever he wants will have to be done on the phone.

"Oh, Mister Sharp, thanks for calling. The Production Company gave me your telephone number, so I left some messages for you."

"About nine, to be exact. What do you want Hershel? If you're looking for phone sex, you've got the wrong number."

"Hah, very funny. It so happens that I have a business proposition for you."

I don't respond. Let's see how he handles the silent treatment.

"Okay, okay, so you don't sound too enthusiastic. Here's what I have in mind. I'd like to sign your client to be my official spokesperson in all my future television commercials. I know she's a little overweight, but the viewers love her. I've been getting more business since that last commercial than I ever thought was possible. Whattaya say? Can we make a deal?"

I tell Hershel that her boyfriend was the movie producer who got killed. He said that he'd heard about that crime, and understands if she'd like some time to get over it. He makes me promise to get back to him in the next couple of weeks, after I've had a chance to discuss it with her.

Every time I walk past Tony's boat, it looks like there's a police convention going on there. He's still on suspension, but all of his police friends are on his side and helping investigate the murder he's charged with. Because the case is an open file with the District Attorney's office, the officers still on duty can justify spending time on it. From the traffic that also reaches our boat, it looks like his investigative team has been instructed to filter all of its findings through the kid, who is a genius at organizing facts that appear to be unrelated, and then connecting the dots to solve a case.

Other than A. Conan Doyle, one of my favorite literary detectives is Rex Stout's Nero Wolfe, the original armchair detective. He was fortunate to have a personal assistant named Archie Goodwin, who did all of his legwork and reported all findings back to his boss, who would then process them through his mental computer and come up with a solution to the crime.

In some ways, Suzi is the modern day Nero Wolfe, but she outdoes him in two ways. First, instead of just one Archie Goodwin, she's got an entire staff of trained professional detectives doing her legwork. And second, in addition to a mental computer, she's got every piece of software known to mankind to help her sort the information. I also have a feeling that as a result of our past involvement with the authorities, she's got copies of all their official law enforcement programs.

Tony finished his scenes on the Venice Soundstage, and Ren tells me that everything went smoothly. They're still shooting some final scenes and post-production should start in another week or so. I've been consulted on courtroom procedures several times, and since my work is now done, our office will be invoicing them for my fee.

Aside from a slight weight loss, you'd never realize that Tony's been charged with murder. I'm reminded of an old saying that goes something like 'sticks and stones can break my bones but names can never hurt me.' Well, that's not entirely true. Of all the names I've been called in my life so far, there's one that really hurts when I hear myself being called it: 'Defendant.'

The majority of people who've never been charged with a crime have difficulty in appreciating the tremendous anxiety and pressure that a defendant feels, but there is one slight example that even the straight and narrow citizens can identify with. It's the feeling you get when a police car's red lights go off in back of you while you're driving down the street at night. The instant you suddenly realize that you're being pulled over because the police think you've done something wrong, the feeling that it's going to cost you time and money to get out of this mess... that's a little what it feels like to be charged with a crime.

In a traffic situation, it's all over in a few minutes, but when you're charged with a serious crime and are facing a trial and possible loss of your freedom, it occupies your thoughts every waking minute of the day, and you desperately hope for something to come along to even momentarily take your mind off of it.

This is why I sympathize with my clients. Civil cases are a little different because the only downside is losing money, but the litigants to those civil cases also feel stressed. Every transaction between human beings carries with it a certain amount of emotion. Some are minor, like a handshake, making a sale, a peck on the cheek or other passing occurrences, but others require more positive or negative emotion. The most stressful are the loss of a loved one, being sued, and being arrested.

Because each client brings a certain amount of emotion along as baggage, it becomes the lawyer's responsibility to sort out what is legal, fair, and reasonable conduct within the judicial system, and what is not.

One prime example is the type of case in which clients may be so emotionally driven that they make unreasonable demands on their attorney are domestic family matters. Separation, Divorce, Property Settlement and Child Custody are the most emotion-ridden matters handled by most lawyers.

There have been more cases of in-court assaults and murders in domestic relations matters than in any other type of case going through the judicial system.

Whenever you hear of a person that goes from one attorney to the other during the course of a legal case, it's probably because they are so driven by emotion that they make unreasonable demands on their lawyer... demands that are ultimately refused, for lack of propriety.

This is why I'm so happy that Tony is handling his arrest and charge of murder so well. If there's anything I don't need, it's an emotional client who carries a gun. We both believe that because there's no way to salvage the bullet that went straight through Joe Caulfield and into a concrete wall, the prosecution might not be able to prove that it came from the empty shell found in Tony's gun. That sounds good to him, and I believe it myself, but neither of us is a ballistics expert, and the smoking gun is still waving in his direction.

The phone rings. It's Myra.

"What's up Mizz Prosecutor? Want to have some dinner with me?"

"No. I'm sorry Peter, but you might want to talk to your client about making a plea on this case."

"Oh please, give me a break. All you've got is a hero cop who was obviously framed. The jury will love him when he gets on the stand. There's no way you can prove that the flattened bullet fragment you found was fired from his gun. That empty shell casing was no doubt planted in his weapon, and you can't even prove that it was fired from his gun. Instead of my considering a plea, you should consider dismissing this entire miscarriage of justice."

"I can see that you don't know much about tool mark identification, Peter."

"Say what? Toolmark identification? What does that have to do with this case? There were no tools used in this murder. Are you holding back on some evidence? You know, as defense attorney I'm entitled to be provided with whatever evidence you have on this case, whether it's exculpatory or not."

"Oh Peter. For goodness sake, calm down. We're not hiding any evidence from you. The purpose of this call is to give you the courtesy of some advance knowledge about what our investigation has turned up. One of our experts has concluded that the spent casing found in your client's weapon wasn't planted there. Not only did it have Tony's fingerprints on it, which establishes the fact that he loaded it, but it also had a matching breech mark to other bullets we test fired from his weapon.

"The people who examine markings on bullets and casings all belong to an organization called AFTE, which stands for Association of Firearms and Toolmarks Examiners, and they not only compare the striations on recovered bullets with rifling marks of guns, they can also analyze 'tool-marks,' the identifying features of fired ammunition.

"When a bullet is fired, a mark is made by the firing pin. The force of the blast then pushes the bullet backwards, causing a breechmark. The toolmark examiners can use those marks to determine whether a spent shell was fired either from a weapon or planted there. In this case, your guy's cannon definitely left its ballistic fingerprint on that empty casing. I'm afraid we've got him, Pete."

"Hold on, genius. All you may have proved is that his gun fired the bullet that left that empty casing. You still haven't shown beyond a reasonable doubt that the bullet fragment scraped off that concrete wall came from the empty shell casing. There's still a hole in your case."

"For God's sake Peter, what do you want from us? A narrated videotape of the shooting? This murder case is no different than most of the others. All we have to do is get enough links in the chain to get a jury to believe the bullet that killed the victim was fired from your guy's gun. And in this case, we've got it. They didn't get along. They had frequent arguments. Your guy has a bad history with people of color. The wound experts will testify that the victim was hit by a .50 caliber bullet. Your guy has a .50 caliber gun that was recently fired. There was a spent shell in his weapon that was definitely fired by that weapon. Case closed. Checkmate. We've got him Pete, and the sooner you realize it, the better it'll be for all of us, including your client.

"Now, because of his distinguished police record, the fact that he may have been provoked during an argument, the heat of passion, yada yada, I'm willing to consider dropping the charge a little. Maybe we can go down to Man 1. Why not talk it over with him?"

My conversation with Myra ends without me mentioning to her that if I suggest to Tony he should consider making a plea even to the reduced charge of manslaughter, I might wind up being the victim in a second count of her murder case. If she's got all the stuff she says she's got, then I've got to invent some new process of ballistic investigation that can show that the empty shell in Tony's gun had been fired at least two or three hours before the police arrived and took his weapon, making it impossible for him to have fired the fatal shot. I admit I've got a really limited knowledge of this ballistic science stuff, but common sense tells me that this will be an impossible task. I'm afraid that Myra actually has found the smoking gun for her jury... and it really was in my client's hand.

10

I arrange to meet with Tony. If he didn't put that empty shell casing in the cylinder of his gun, then someone else must have planted it there. Forget the ballistics junk. All we have to do is find anyone who might have had access to his gun. The time frame is even nicely narrowed down for us. He claims that he was on the range firing that day, so the casing must have been planted between when he finished firing, and the time he entered the soundstage. That's only a window of about two hours, so now it's time for him to relive every minute of that period, and we may find out who our killer is.

Tony's preliminary hearing date is rapidly approaching, so we've got some work to do. A good thing about Tony being a cop is that he's testified in hundreds of prelims. He won't be testifying in this one, but I don't have to make the same explanation to him that most clients require.

If the prosecution wants to bring a person to trial on a felony charge In the State of California, they have two choices: Indictment or Information. With an indictment, they go before the Grand Jury. If that group returns a 'bill of indictment,' it's then straight to the Superior Court for arraignment and trial. Like so many others, this case will be going by Information, which means a preliminary hearing first, at which time the prosecution doesn't have to establish guilt on the part of the defendant. All they have to do is establish that a crime has been committed and that there is reasonable cause to believe that the defendant may have been involved. The defendant is then 'bound over' for arraignment and trial in the Superior Court.

Defense attorneys don't put up any fight at a preliminary hearing, because all they want to do is see the prosecution's case and try to pick it apart, looking for weak spots. Quite often a criminal client will be disappointed that their attorney didn't do more for them at the prelim, but Tony knows that a prelim is the prosecutor's show, and I'm glad it is, because I don't have any kind of show to put on for Tony.

If all the investigations come up dry, Tony's trial will be a terrible disaster. Tony knows this too. I try to cheer him up a little. "You know Tony, the prosecution has the burden of proof. They've got to show beyond a reasonable doubt that you shot Joe Caulfield. You're innocent until they prove you guilty, and I intend to make that as difficult as I can for them."

His response is not what I expected.

"You really believe that crap don't you? You think that the prosecution thinks the same way? Listen here counselor, I was found guilty the minute they opened my weapon and found that empty shell casing. The only purpose of this trial is to give me a chance to prove that I'm innocent. I'm afraid you've got the phrase backwards.

"I've been a cop long enough to know that the cops and prosecutors don't have the time or ingenuity to railroad innocent people for crimes they didn't commit. Sure there's the rare exception of a bad cop or D.A. who'll fabricate testimony, but I've never seen it happen here in L.A. County, so as far as I'm concerned, it's not happening. There was no big conspiracy in the O.J. case, and there's none here either. I've brought cases to the D.A.'s office on plenty of occasions and gotten 'rejects,' because they didn't think they had a dead-bang winner.

"The D.A., the judge, the jury, and probably you, all think I blew Joe Caulfield away, and that's why I've got a whole team of good buddies working around the clock trying to find out who really did it. They're the only ones I can count on. They're the only ones who really believe I'm innocent, and your little kid is one of them.

"You're a professional, so I know you'll do your best for me whether you believe I'm innocent or not, but you should stop once in a while and ask yourself what you really believe about me. Am I innocent until proven guilty, or is it the other way around?"

Tony doesn't mince words. There aren't a lot of places his thoughts go through on that trip from his brain to his mouth. I appreciate him for being honest with me about his feelings, and am afraid to say that he's right about everything he just said, with one exception. I do believe that he's innocent of this murder.

The phone rings: I see Snell's number on the caller ID display.

"Special Agent Snell. How nice of you to call your favorite undercover agent. What can I do for you today?"

"You're not an undercover agent. You're not an agent of any kind. You're a cooperating witness, and the purpose of this call is to thank your little girl for letting us know that those other two DVD's you ordered came in at your private mailbox place. She authorized the clerk over there to allow one of our lab people to pick them up.

"The postmark on the first one you received was from the San Pedro district, but these two look like they'd been mailed from Van Nuys, so I guess they move around a lot to avoid bringing any attention to themselves in the local post offices. All we know for sure now is that even though the website and bank accounts are probably overseas, the main operation must be right here in town.

"Oh, and one other thing. We did happen to find a useable fingerprint on one of the DVD discs. After sending it through every law enforcement database, we came up with a match. It was the guy your client wasted. Joseph Caulfield. Any idea how it could have gotten there?"

This opens up a whole new line of investigation for me, and for once I've got some information that the kid doesn't know about. Racking my brain for any relevant fact that could possibly help on this case, I put together what looks to me like a reasonable theory, and just to see how it holds up, I try it out by explaining it. Unfortunately, the only audience I can put together on short notice is Suzi's Saint Bernard, but he's proven to be a pretty good listener in the past, so he qualifies.

First, the main two reasons that people get killed are love and money. I don't think that Joe was involved in any love triangle, so I'm checking off 'money' in the motive box.

Second, his fingerprint appeared on a bootlegged DVD, so he might probably be involved in the piracy scheme. But if he was a bad guy, then he would have been doing the shooting, instead of being on the receiving end, so he must be a good guy. And if he's a good guy, then he may have gotten killed because he stumbled onto what the bad guys were doing.

Joe mentioned that he was starting up a company that would do secure transportation and babysitting of first run motion picture prints. He therefore must have plenty of connections with people who move those prints around, and any one of them could be part of the piracy gang. It also answers the question as to how his fingerprints got into the 'system.' You have to get printed to be bonded, and the new film delivery company needed a bond.

Unlike those guys with patches over one eye and a peg leg, motion picture pirates don't jump from one boat to another with swords drawn, but I wouldn't put it past one of them to whack someone who got in the way of their profitable operation.

At this point I don't really know much about how movies are shuttled around, so I take a short trip over to the multiplex in our neighborhood and pick the theater manager's brain. She tells me that the films are usually delivered at least a day or so before they're to be shown. This lead time is for the projectionist to take the several reels that the film is on and splice them together, so that they can run through the projector continuously. They call this 'building the film,' and it eliminates the old practice that required 'changing reels' every fifteen or twenty minutes. I learn that an experienced projectionist can splice the reels together on a specially designed table in less than fifteen minutes - and that includes adding in the trailers for upcoming films.

A film might stay at a theater for a full week or more. When it's not being projected it stays on the table, all in one continuous piece, in between showings. After the theater is done with it, the projectionist breaks down the 'build' and puts the numerous reels back into their original containers. They're then brought down to the manager's office to be ready for pickup by Airborne, UPS, or a studio messenger service. The manager thinks that each reel contains about two thousand feet of film. My conversation with people at the Venice Soundstage educated me to the fact that 35 millimeter film goes through a projector at about ninety feet a minute, so two thousand feet of film should provide about eighteen safe, useable minutes. This would make the average film at least a five or six-reel movie.

The containers that the manager showed me contain three reels each, so most movies probably fit into two or three containers, which would give an average film a running time of up to about two hours.

I also know that the Venice Soundstage's manager Renaldo has another job: he's a projectionist. This means that he has access to film prints and also knows how to 'build' a film by splicing the reels together. And he also must know how to 'unsplice' the reels, to remove one for some homework.

If Renaldo can unsplice the built film and take one reel out each evening, he can conceivably copy it and then bring it back and re-splice it in the next day. Now that I've got the mechanical part of the operation together in my mind, I think I may have the rest of the puzzle too. Joe Caulfield must have accidentally discovered Renaldo's sideline career of piracy. He probably stumbled onto a stash of counterfeit DVD's, called Renaldo on it, and threatened to expose the whole operation. There was no other choice: Joe had to be eliminated before he could go to the cops. This means that Renaldo is the killer. I still don't know how he could have gotten that empty casing into Tony's gun, but I'm working on it. The dog is now lying down, so I better wrap this presentation up while his eyes are still open.

Unfortunately, Renaldo was working at the theater when Joe was shot, so he's got a good alibi. Someone else must have done the killing for him. I still don't know who that someone is, but I'm positive that it wasn't Tony. All I've got to do now is get Tony's gang to do an around-the-clock surveillance of Joe's movements, and we'll find out who he's working with - and probably who killed Joe. The dog is now snoring.

This has been a productive day. Not only have I solved Snell's piracy case for him, but I've also found out why Joe Caulfield was killed, and I'm now on the way to proving who did it and then framed Tony.

11

Tony's preliminary hearing is being handled by one of Myra's deputy prosecutors. This means that she must think this case is going to be an easy winner and her presence isn't required. Unfortunately, she's right. All I've got now is some unproven theories with absolutely nothing to support them.

Tony's case is called and the deputy D.A. goes through the case right by the numbers. First, the coroner establishes that a crime has been committed by bringing in his autopsy report, showing that the victim died as the result of being shot by a large caliber weapon. About the only thing I can do to this witness is get him to admit that the wound might have possibly been made by a .357 or .44 magnum bullet. This slightly distracts from the concentration on .50 caliber ammunition, but probably not too much.

Next to the witness stand is the first responding officer. He testifies to the fact that Tony was there, and after identifying himself, peacefully surrendered his weapon. Their lab tech testifies to the fact that Tony's gun had recently been fired, and it contained one spent round in the cylinder that had Tony's fingerprints on it. They also show that the breech mark on the spent round matches breech marks on other test rounds fired from Tony's gun.

An embarrassed witness who worked with the film company testifies to the fact that Tony had numerous arguments with the victim. This witness is obviously having a rough time doing this, because I notice that he can't look Tony in the eye.

Having established enough Means, Opportunity and Motive, the judge has no other choice but the binding of Tony over for arraignment and trial. A date is set for his next appearance up in the Superior Court, and we now have less than a month to find the real killer.

I explain my piracy theory to Tony and suggest that at trial we nail Renaldo for his bootlegging of movies, and arrange to have Special Agent Snell arrest Renaldo right there in court, in front of the jury. Then, when my cross examination and arguments turn to the theory of Joe being killed because he stumbled onto Renaldo's illegal activities, maybe we can create some reasonable doubt in the minds of at least one juror... and that's all it takes. As usual, he doesn't show any emotion.

Back at the boat, we discuss some of the results his investigators have already come up with. I'm particularly interested in whatever they've found about Joe Caulfield and Renaldo Zeti, the projectionist pirate, and my main suspect.

Nothing stands out in Joe Caulfield's folder. He's a hard working guy who graduated with a degree in film production and worked his way up from production assistant to producer in less than ten years. He's never been in the system, and if it wasn't for the fact that we had his fingerprints as a victim and applicant for the bonded courier service he wanted to start, we never would have been able to tie him into the piracy gang.

His love life consisted of two or three relationships with morbidly obese white women, which may explain how he wound up with April. His hobbies included screenwriting, playing guitar, and shooting. This is no surprise because Tony mentioned that he and one of the people in the film company were on the target range together. I was hoping that it was Renaldo, because that may have been where the empty casing was planted in Tony's gun. Unfortunately, that part of my theory is now down the toilet. The folder also says that Joe had his own apartment, but spent several nights a week over at April's place.

Not one of the other members of the stage's film company had anything in their files that would cast any suspicion on them. Not all of them were angels, but a bust for possession of funny cigarettes or drunk driving doesn't necessarily lead to piracy and murder. Each one of them were also asked about alibis for the period of time when they wrapped on the day of the murder, to the time that Tony discovered Joe's body, and every one of them had an alibi that checked out. Renaldo didn't do it. Nobody did it. Tony says this isn't unusual in a murder investigation, but it certainly seems unusual to me.

While we're going through the files, I happen to notice the one on Evelyn's daughter. She's in her early twenties, so she really hasn't had any time to get into trouble. Her file is almost empty. Certainly no criminal past, not even a speeding ticket. Her only problem had been getting thrown out of acting classes for non-payment of tuition. A check of the civil cases in our jurisdiction showed that several acting schools had sued her, but that ultimately, they

162

were all paid in full and the cases were dismissed during the past year. And, as her mother told me, the investigation confirms that her father died in an accident five years ago.

My main suspect is still Renaldo Zeti, so I ask Tony to go over that file with me. I know that Suzi has all these folders in her computer, but my piracy theory is something that she doesn't know about yet, unless the dog told her, which is highly unlikely because he was nodding off through most of my presentation.

Ren lives upstairs of the soundstage. He also went to film school, and because it's the same school that Joe attended, that's probably where they met. Unlike Joe, Ren didn't have the drive that it takes to advance in the entertainment industry. Maybe he didn't have the talent either. Ren's family owns the building where the Venice Soundstage is, and when they passed away he inherited it.

The property is a valuable asset because soundstage rental can be many thousands of dollars a month, so Ren probably just wasn't hungry enough to work his way up the production ladder. His outside job of projectionist, along with some steady rental income from the soundstage, and a built-in job as production assistant must have been enough to satisfy him for a while... until he got greedy and decided to become a pirate.

Tony's surveillance team also liked Ren for Joe's murder, so they had him covered starting the day after the murder. There was no lead to any co-conspirators. Ren worked on the stage all day every day, and left early a couple of nights each week to go to the multiplex theater, where he performed his projectionist duties and came right back home.

The reports didn't mention anything about whether Ren was carrying a package when he left for the theater or returned home, so Tony changed their instructions and added the requirement that he be photographed if he's seen carrying anything. The stakeout team agreed, and got their camera equipment ready, complete with night vision lenses.

Without further reports from Tony's investigators, there's not much I can do on the case. Since I've probably got it all figured out, I might as well turn everything over to the kid. I prepare a written report containing my evidence and theories and tuck it into the dog's collar. This is the most direct means of communication we've got on our boat.

There's a lull in the action on Tony's case until his investigation team reports, so I call April to see how she's doing. She tells me that time will heal everything, and that she's started to religiously follow a weight loss program that has completely changed her lifestyle. She has become a vegetarian, eats a lot of fresh fruits and vegetables, and has started on a moderate walking program, all with her doctor's approval. During the past few weeks, she's already lost almost twenty pounds, and plans to continue eating healthy and exercising for the rest of her life. I'm really glad to hear this.

As for business, April has resigned from the phone sex operation and is now a model. Hershel Belsky got tired of waiting for me to get back to him. He was getting so many requests for April from the viewers of his commercials, that he went around me to contact her directly. When he offered her a nice salary just to occasionally drive a car past Hershel while he was on camera making a commercial, she decided to accept. I make a mental note to set my TIVO to record a late night movie, just to see April in one of Hershel's commercials.

After I hang up the phone, there's a knock on the hull. It's the messenger service delivering some paperwork from Myra's office. I see that it contains copies of all the witness statements they took. By law, the defense is entitled to see them. Also enclosed is a copy of their witness list for the trial. Nothing out of the ordinary except for one name at the bottom of the list: Suzi Braunstien.

I know that Suzi and Myra talk on the phone at least once every day, but can't believe that the kid would ever reveal to Myra any details about our defense. I call Myra's office. She answers her private line.

"You got my package, huh?"

"Yes, I got your package and I want to know what you're doing."

"What do you mean?"

"You know exactly what I mean. I saw her name at the bottom of the list. You can't be serious. You don't want her testifying in a murder case. She's only a kid."

"Peter, she may only be a kid, but let's face it, she's got more brainpower than you and me combined and besides, I have no other choice."

"How can you have no other choice? She's a member of the defense team. You know what she does here. She's the computer expert for all our evidence. She puts the whole case together. You can't possibly expect the judge to allow you to ask her about privileged communications she's had with me, or our investigators, or our client. What can you possibly expect to learn from her?"

"Calm down, Peter. The reason I had no choice other than to subpoena her is because there was more than one set of prints on that empty shell casing we found in Tony's gun. The second set of prints matched Suzi's."

The thing that really surprises me here is that Myra had something to compare Suzi's prints to.

"Myra, I'm going to ask you only one question, and I pray to God that your answer isn't what I'm afraid it might be. How did you know that those prints belonged to Suzi?"

"Oh Peter, wake up. Are you afraid that I got her prints off of my computer at the house? Is that what's bothering you? That I snuck around to try and nail her for something? Don't be silly. Her prints were in the system for a whole bunch of reasons. Let's see now, one time was when she immigrated to this country. Another time was when she tried to apply for volunteer work with the L.A.P.D. as an Eagle Scout, and then again when she became a home-schooled student. And another time was when she sent in her application for early admission to Harvard Law School, and those results were just on our first search. Need I continue? She's been fingerprinted more times than you have, and she's never been arrested.

"And the reason why I had to subpoena her as a witness was because the only other alternative was to add her as a possible co-defendant. You know that

I could never do that, so I'm afraid she's on the list, and that's final.

"I know about the privileges involved in matters like this, and I assure you that the only questions that she'll be asked are about her fingerprints on that casing, and nothing else. In fact, I won't even be doing the asking. One of my deputies will be taking this case to trial. I may pop in on the day that Suzi's on the stand, but otherwise, I'm keeping out of this one."

There's no sense my telling the kid about her name being on the prosecution's witness list, because I know that Myra wouldn't have done it without explaining it to her first. Tony told me that he taught the kid how to use his reloading press, and I'm sure that Myra knows it too, because that's the only way those little prints could have gotten there. Myra's correct. If it ever came out that the kid's prints were on the shell casing and the matter wasn't followed up on there would be a full investigation, and none of us wants one of those. I'm also sure Myra doesn't think Suzi planted that casing in there.

I know this whole thing can't be easy for the kid. On one hand, she's deeply involved in trying to work with the defense team in trying to clear our client, who is also a neighbor and friend of hers. On the other hand, the only way she can help to win this case is by causing the defeat of Myra's office, and I know that the kid idolizes her. Not an easy choice, and I know it. I face it every time I go up against our District Attorney.

Evelyn is calling. She wants to get together with me again, but under the existing circumstances of her being a possible suspect in a criminal conspiracy, I can't. And I don't know how to tell her. The truth of the matter is that her daughter is part of the film company, and until we find out how many other people Ren might be working with, everyone from production assistants to the producer is under suspicion.

Not only do I want to avoid hurting her feelings by hinting that her daughter is a possible suspect, but I can't take the chance of tipping our hand about the piracy operation. If she were to tell her daughter and the word got out, then our whole investigation would be ruined. The bad guys would fold up their tent and disappear, and we'd lose the tiny advantage we now have of knowing what's going on without them being aware of it. We need that gang desperately, to take the heat off of Tony. That gang is my 'go-to' suspect, my only way to try and create reasonable doubt of Tony's guilt.

I don't want to lie to her, so I tell her that I'm in the middle of a capital case and every waking moment must be devoted to it, because a client's life is at stake. She says that she understands, and asks me how the investigation is going. This doesn't sit well with me. It can mean that she's sincerely interested in my work, or that she wants to know how close we may be to nailing the bad guys because her daughter might be one of them. I give her the benefit of the doubt and thank her for her concern about my case. She seems to appreciate the fact that I'm not at liberty to discuss any of the details, so we both agree to get together after the case is finished. I suggest we try Pollo Meshuga again, but she's got a better idea: if I win, she'd prefer the Lahaina Yacht Club on

Maui. Boy, I sure hope I win this case. This may wind up being the best contingency fee any lawyer ever collected.

Every time I get involved with a bright, attractive, solvent female, it seems like the relationship is cursed. Some reason always pops up that makes our future together impossible. It's like the kid is putting some invisible hex on any woman except Myra. But not this time. The kid doesn't even know Evelyn's name, how I met her or anything about her. And neither does Myra. Keeping those two relationship saboteurs out of the loop may give me a chance with Evelyn. I'm going to give this one a chance to take its normal course, without any outside influence from the Suzi-Myra conspiracy.

The around-the-clock surveillance of Renaldo is unproductive, but the team did manage to get some photos of him carrying a briefcase when he went to work, and also when returning to his apartment over the soundstage.

I ask Tony about the rear exit from the soundstage building. He seems surprised.

"What do you mean the rear exit? There's no door back there, just a set of double doors that open to allow equipment trucks to come in and out. You can't think that…"

He stops himself before finishing his sentence and grabs his cell phone, quickly dialing a number.

"This is Tony. I want an extra team on the soundstage, whenever it's closed for business after the shooting day ends. The second team should cover the drive-in door in the alley. And I want pictures too." Nobody's perfect, and that includes Tony. He just remembered that back way is how he entered the soundstage the night of Joe's murder. All this time, neither one of us thought to cover it because it's rarely used for regular comings and goings.

Tony explains to his teams that there's a possibility someone may have been using the back doors while the surveillance team was parked outside watching the front door to the soundstage, and Renaldo's car parked on the street. This never occurred to them before, because there's nothing particular within walking distance of the place, and they figured that if Ren was going anywhere, that he would take his car.

We have to wait another couple of days before anything develops, but the alley team does come up with something. Between three and four in the morning, there was some activity in the alley. The back doors to the soundstage open and a vehicle pulled in. Less than an hour later, while it was still dark outside, the same vehicle left. When it happened again the next night, the team was ready with a third 'tail' unit standing by. It was composed of another cop who was driving a taxicab that Tony's team borrowed from one of their snitches so that the cop/cab driver could follow the suspect vehicle. I thought it was pretty clever their using a cab for the tail, because it's such a common sight, that even a paranoid person would have difficulty in thinking that a cab behind them was actually a tail. And at that hour of the morning, cabs are probably the most common vehicles on the street.

The cab's report comes in first. The vehicle left the soundstage, drove to the South Los Angeles suburb of Compton, and proceeded to stop at every mailbox in that neighborhood, dropping some small packages in each one.

As far as I'm concerned, this nails down the piracy case, because that vehicle is obviously doing the mailings of DVDs to customers. The upsetting part of the report is when the alley team's photos come in. They used a digital camera and a wireless Internet connection to e-mail us the photographs. At first I didn't want to believe it, but there was a match when they ran the license plates. The registration showed up a name that was familiar to me. So was the feeling. The car belongs to Evelyn.

12

I hate getting shot down like this again. The team's photos don't identify the driver any further than establishing the sex as being female, but whether it's Evelyn or her starlet daughter doesn't really matter to me anymore, because the result will be the same. This is another relationship that's over. At least I've avoided the embarrassment of having been warned about her in advance by Suzi and Myra. Without knowing it, they have one less relationship failure of mine to gloat over.

We have a strategy meeting about how to handle this new evidence. If the guys pick up the driver, she'll probably want to make a deal by pleading that it's just a night job and she has no idea what's in the packages. Even if she gives us Renaldo, that's not good enough. We still won't know how far up the food chain this gang goes, and Renaldo can claim that he was upstairs sleeping all night and had no idea that someone was breaking in the rear doors of the soundstage, probably with a stolen set of keys.

If this ring is to be broken, we've got to find out everyone involved and how the actual piracy is being done. We're unanimous on two decisions. First, we follow through and find out more about the operation. And second, we absolutely don't bring Snell and the FBI into it. The last thing we need now is a bunch of guys in SWAT uniforms swarming in the soundstage, with news cameras filming the big 'FBI' emblems on the backs of their jackets. We're not interested in publicity here, and our main concern isn't busting a piracy gang. We want to find out who murdered Joe Caulfield. Anything else that comes out of it is pure gravy.

I still have a problem believing that Evelyn is involved. If she doesn't know that her daughter is using her car, the FBI's prosecution won't be my fault, and I might be able to salvage the relationship.

Tony opens his file on the daughter, and then it hits me. According to Evelyn, after her husband was killed in that helicopter, they came into a sizeable settlement from the helicopter company. That was supposed to have happened at least five years ago, but just a year ago the daughter was tossed out of several acting schools for failure to pay her tuition. That raises the question of why the bills weren't paid if there was plenty of money around.

One of Tony's guys prepared a supplemental report. Evelyn's husband was killed in a helicopter accident all right, but it wasn't the helicopter manufacturer's fault. He was drunk and fell out of the chopper as it was landing. There was a lawsuit, but the helicopter company won and didn't have to pay anything to widow Evelyn.

This evidence tells us that they were poor a few years ago, and are quite well off now. We also know that it hasn't been as a result of the daughter's career, because she's only made minimum scale on the couple of low budget pictures she's worked on recently. So where did the money come from to pay off her lawsuits, get some nice clothes, a nice place to live, and a nice car to drive? Evelyn doesn't have a job, so the money's got to be coming in from somewhere.

I take a closer look at the supplemental report on Evelyn's late husband and see that he was working for a company that manufactured equipment for the entertainment industry. His job was to demonstrate and sell a special piece of equipment called a 'Telecine.' What a coincidence. I just happen to know where one of those things is.

A friend of mine works at one of the major motion picture studios, so I call and ask him what a Telecine does. His answer clears up a lot of questions. That particular machine is used to transfer motion picture film to videotape, that can then be used for computer editing…or to make DVD's.

At this point we probably have enough to get a search warrant for the soundstage. From what we've put together, here's how the operation runs: Ren un-splices one or two reels a night from the projectionist booth, brings them back to the soundstage, and then spends the next couple of hours using the Telecine for transferring the film to a master videotape. The next day he returns those reels to the booth and brings home others that night and repeats the same operation until he's got the entire film copied onto some format that can be used to make bootlegged copies.

Their next step is to add the new available title to their website and then use a bunch of DVD burners to make product for filling their orders. When they verify that the direct bank transfers have been made, the videos and DVD's are packaged, addressed, stamped, and made ready for mailing. Whoever drives the delivery SUV pulls into the rear doors of the soundstage to get loaded up, and then goes on a countywide mailbox run.

This is a neat little operation, but still begs the question of why kill Joe? From what the alley surveillance team saw, there were less than fifty packages mailed each night. According to their website, they only make about twenty dollars a package, so this means that on a steady basis, there's only about a thousand dollars a night coming in. That's a nice extra income for any average person, but if there are three or four people involved, that means all they've done is create a decent living wage for themselves, by working all night, and breaking some Federal laws. Hardly enough to kill a guy for.

If their little scheme got off the ground with the formation of that motion picture film courier service, they might get a crack at some of the big budget premieres and sneak previews. With titles like that, they could charge twice as much, and sell much more, raising the potential income to a level of maybe five to ten thousand a night. They wouldn't be able to drive around and find mailboxes at night for all of the orders, but they'd no doubt figured out how to overcome that problem.

Another unanimous decision is that Joe wasn't killed for stumbling onto the business. In all probability he was in on it, and was planning on using his connections in the industry to start the courier system up so that they could get direct access to the motion picture films and make some really big money. They needed him for that connection, so why kill him? I reluctantly agree that he may have been involved with the gang, but still have difficulty in believing it myself.

There's a knock on our hull. Looking over the side, I see that it's some guy wearing a tie. Ordinarily, I would just let him know that I don't need any insurance today and send him on his merry way, but this is my courteous day of the week. Without inviting him aboard, I try to find out why he's bothering me.

"What can I do for you?"

He looks at his wristwatch. "I have an appointment with Doctor Braunstien."

This is a new twist. I know she intends to attend Harvard Law School and ultimately partner up with Myra, but I didn't know that she became a doctor of anything while I was asleep last night. I might as well ask the main question, just to gauge the level of surprise that this sucker is in for.

"Have you had the pleasure of meeting the good doctor before today?"

"No I haven't, but several of our law enforcement customers speak highly of her, and I know that she's a very young, bright person."

I motion for him to come aboard. He gets his first surprise when the dog comes out to meet him.

"My goodness, that's an attractive large animal."

"That's not an animal, that's the doctor's associate, Igor. Just walk that way. He'll take you to the doctor's laboratory."

They both disappear into the forward stateroom and the door closes behind them. This completely shuts me out of whatever they're doing, but that's the way things are around here. I handle the courtroom part of our business any way that I want to, and she takes care of the office operation. We're sort of a Mister Outside, Miss Inside kind of team. There are things she does that are beyond my comprehension, and there are things I do that she has no ability to understand, like getting arrested for crimes, getting involved with female criminals, screwing up my marriage to Myra, and other complicated stuff not designed to be appreciated by kids like her.

After about an hour in there, Mister Necktie is led out by Igor. I can't help but notice that there's something that looks familiar sticking out of the guy's folder case. If my first glance is correct, it's one of our law firm's checks.

Ordinarily, I let her do anything she wants, but when our money is being spent, my curiosity is aroused. There's no way I would ever second-guess her decision to spend our money, but this time I'd at least like to have some idea of what it's for, so I stop him with a smile and offer him a seat on the couch, letting him know that he's got at least another hour or so before the traffic starts to get heavy. I'd like to know what we've purchased, but I also want to avoid looking too stupid.

"So, how did your meeting with the doctor go today?"

"Oh, quite nicely. You're Mister Peter Sharp, the well known criminal attorney, aren't you?"

That's it. I already like this guy. I modestly nod, letting him know that his exceptional powers of observation are correct. He goes on.

"Recognizing people and objects is my life. It's what I do for a living, and I like to think I'm pretty good at it."

It looks like this guy has no problem with modesty holding him back. The check in his folder seems to have given him a lot more confidence than he had when first coming aboard, so he goes on.

"On behalf of our entire organization, I want to thank you for your order, and to let you know that you are now in position to be a leading forensic science firm."

He has a wonderful way of talking without saying anything that I'm really interested in. All I want to know now is 'what the hell did we buy, and how much did we spend for it?'

"On behalf of Doctor Braunstien and myself, I accept your thanks. When can we expect delivery?" I still haven't exactly asked him what we bought, but maybe his answer to my delivery question will lead to the subject matter.

"Oh, it's already here. Because it's only software, once I received your check, I went to our website, entered the proper authorization code, and gave your office access to the downloading process."

He looks at his wristwatch. "Depending on the width of your broadband connection, I'd say that it should be completely downloaded in two or three minutes."

I take another shot at getting some explanation of what we just paid for. "Do you think we'll have any trouble operating the program? I mean, does your firm offer any technical support if we have a problem? Is there a toll-free customer support number we can call?"

"Oh, I don't think you'll have any problem with that. The doctor obviously has had experience in the past, working with local law enforcement

178

agencies. She knows quite a bit about how to operate both the Facial Recognition and Toolmark Identification segments. I don't know why she wanted both *Drug-Fire* and *IBIS*, but she must have some need for them both."

Being the expert he is, he obviously recognizes that I haven't the slightest idea of what he's talking about, so he decides to put me out of my misery. "*Drug-Fire* was developed in part by the FBI, and is computerized technology that allows one to investigate and compare characteristics of expended cartridges with others, and those in the law enforcement computer system. Its database has been online since September of 1995 and contains thousands of cartridges and bullets. The system you now have here is also installed in hundreds of crime labs worldwide, is used by almost a thousand firearms examiners and technicians, and has processed close to one hundred thousand cases worldwide.

"*IBIS* is an acronym for Integrated Ballistics Identification System and was developed by our ATF. The program is also known as '*Bulletproof*' and '*Brass Catcher,*' and has been online since July of 1996. Between those two systems, your office is now on the leading edge of Toolmark Identification and Ballistic Fingerprinting.

"*MANDRAKE,* Face ID, Face It and *Imagis' ID-2000* are the leading products in computerized 2-D facial recognition software. *ILEFIS,* the 3-D program, isn't ready for distribution yet, but when it comes out, your office will be one of the first to have it. I left a beta version of it for her to try out. It works by focusing on 64 facial features, like a chin, nose, lower lip, or eye. The researchers have identified as many as 256 unique shapes for each of the features, and the software program uses a set of numbers, like a number 21 nose, a number 32 eye socket, and a number 34 lip. What we wind up with is a numerical face code.

"Security cameras scan the peaks and valleys of features, called 'nodal points.' The human face contains over 80 nodal points, but only 14 to 22 stable nodal points are needed for a successful match. Stable nodal points are those that don't fluctuate with weight or expression, like eye socket depth.

"So there you have it. Your forensics section is now one of the best equipped ones in the country, and the law enforcement agencies that referred us to you will no doubt be paying for your services soon, on a consultant basis."

So that's it. The kid bought some detective software. Why, I still don't know, but being the ultimate armchair sleuth that she is, I'm sure it will come in handy. I hate to do it, but I've got to ask one more question.

"By the way, just so I can keep track of our finances, what did the total of that check come to?"

Mister necktie has been gone for about a half hour, and I'm still sitting here in shock. I'm no computer expert, but I appreciate the value of good software programs. When the guy told me how many thousands of dollars we just spent, it really surprised me. In the past, the kid has never charged anything for helping out her cop friends, but maybe she can get hooked up with some private labs and start getting fees for us.

I go to the galley, get out the dog biscuit box, and shake it. If Bernie is anywhere within about a half mile radius, it'll get him front and center in less than a minute, and this time it only took about four seconds. I reward his attendance with one of the biscuits, and tuck a note into his collar with only one question on it: "Dr. Braunstien, did we really have to spend that much money on the software?"

It only takes a few minutes before I get a response to my dogmail. The reply note has only one sentence on it. "If it doesn't work to solve any of the cases we're now working on and pay for itself by the end of the year, then the total cost will come out of my end." Well, I guess that tells me something. I tip the messenger with the customary pat on the head and 'good boy' compliment, and he returns to his home base.

Next to Stuart, Suzi is the sharpest businessperson I've ever encountered. For her to offer payment of this software out of her portion of the firm's income, she must be pretty sure that it'll pay off on our cases. Unfortunately our only open one is Tony's, which I believe is a no-fee job. Suzi gets so much help from the local cops, that whenever they have a problem, she offers our services. Most of the time all we have to do is help fill out paperwork for different things like divorces, retirement, and auto accidents, but this time we got stuck on a murder defense. I'm sure the kid will figure some way for us to wind up getting money out of this case. She usually does. And if I know her at all, she's already got driver's license photos in her computer for every person that Tony's team talked to. The kid stayed at Myra's house recently while I was vacationing in the

La Verne City Jail, so she no doubt she now also has Myra's law enforcement passwords and can access all of the criminal records databases usually reserved for use by cops only.

It's nice to know how well equipped our modest law firm is. With this new knowledge I feel relaxed enough to sit back, flip on the flat panel television screen, and watch the Dodgers pre-game show.

The local news practice of 'if it bleeds, it leads' seems to have worked its way into sports coverage too, because they open the show with news of a dead body that was found in the trunk of a car in the parking lot of Dodger Stadium. He couldn't have been a ticket scalper, because the Blue Crew hasn't been doing so well lately and there's no problem getting a seat at one of their home games.

The phone rings. It's Stuart calling. I don't even have time to say hello, because as soon as I take the phone off the hook, I hear his excited voice.

"Peter, you've got to meet me this afternoon. I got a phone call from the FBI. They want me to come in to their West Los Angeles office. I'm supposed to be there in two hours. Please, can you meet me there?"

13

I haven't the slightest idea why the FBI wants to talk to Stuart, but it can only be for one of the two things he's currently involved in that touches on their jurisdiction. Either his Thai girls import service or his interstate gambling scheme. Whichever one it might be that raised their curiosity, it's unlikely they'd call him in to talk about it, because that's not the way they work. Their usual method is to first build up an airtight case against their suspect and then with the television cameras watching, storm his office and take him away in handcuffs. That's a lot more fun for them, and gets more press coverage.

"Calm down, Stuart. Did they tell you anything about why they want you to come in?"

"Yes, they said they'd like my assistance in a case they're looking into. That means I'm not in trouble, right? All they need is my help. Right?"

"Wrong. The FBI doesn't need your help, Stuart. They don't need anyone's help. They've got a big budget and plenty of employees. If they need your help, it's only to give them enough information to arrest you for something."

Stuart doesn't respond. "Listen, Stuart, I'll meet you there, but in the event that you get there before I do, it's imperative that you don't say anything to anyone. You know that warning they give people who get arrested? The one that has words like 'anything you say can and will be used against you?' Well they really mean it. Don't say a word to anyone unless I let you know that it's okay."

"Peter, I really appreciate this, I mean your meeting me on such short notice. I want you to know that your meter will be running from the time we hang up the phone. Is that okay?"

"No Stuart, it's not okay. The meter started running when I picked up the phone."

With all of his business enterprises running so successfully, Stuart is doing quite well now. He's scared out of his wits, and that's the best kind of client to have, because when they're that scared, they have more of a tendency to hide behind you and let you run things the way you see fit.

The Marina is about fifteen miles closer to the West Los Angeles Federal Building than Stuart's office is, so I'm having no difficulty in getting there before he arrives. I give my card to the receptionist and in just a few minutes one of Snell's drones comes out to escort me back to his boss' office. When attaching a visitor's pass to my pocket, I ask the agent to tell the receptionist to please call Snell's office when Stuart arrives.

As usual, Snell is not very excited to see me.

"Hello Sharp, what brings you in here today? I hope it's to give me some additional info on that movie piracy gang."

"Not quite. You called a client of mine and asked him to come in this afternoon. For some strange reason he felt intimidated by your request, so he asked me to hold his hand while you try to beat some information out of him."

"Very funny, but he really doesn't have that much to worry about, because it's a murder that we're investigating, and in no way do we like him for the actual crime. We do think that he's had some connection with the victim, and that's why we want to talk to him."

"That's interesting. I didn't know that the FBI investigated murders in this town. Isn't that local police business?"

Our friendly chat is interrupted by Snell's intercom. He picks up his phone, gets the message, and nods at his assistant, who then leaves the room.

"Your client is here."

Stuart is led into the office and he's as white as a ghost. He sits down in a chair next to me and the look on his face tells me that he's too frightened to talk. Snell starts in.

"Mister Schwartzman, are you acquainted with a man named Joey the Flange?"

Stuart doesn't answer. He just sits there, frozen.

"The reason I'm asking if you know him, is because we found your name and number in his personal belongings. To be quite honest, Mister Schwarzman, Mister Flange is the name of a dead person who was discovered in the trunk of a car parked outside of Dodger Stadium - a car trunk that had stolen New Jersey license plates on it. Now we all know that a car trunk isn't usually where a person who dies of natural causes would be, so the location of his final resting place, along with the small caliber bullet hole in the back of his skull has led our top notch lab technicians to believe that there may have been some foul play involved in his untimely death. So, I repeat, are you acquainted with him?"

I didn't think it was possible, but Stuart is now whiter than he was when first coming into Snell's office. With so much blood drained out of his face, I'm afraid he might pass out any time now, so I interrupt the friendly chat.

"Stuart, you don't look so good. Why don't you come over here and relax on the couch?"

Snell knows exactly what I'm doing, because he also noticed how white Stuart was getting. As much as the FBI loves publicity, I don't think they're looking for the kind that they'd get if a witness dies in their office as the result of a stroke that occurs during a friendly chat. Snell motions for his assistant to get Stuart a glass of water and then makes the smart decision of directing the rest of his conversation directly to me.

"Sharp, people in law enforcement don't like coincidences popping up, and there have been so many in this case, that they're just impossible to ignore. First, we have reason to believe that Mister Flange was involved in some illegal activity in his office building, like the selling of drugs, or bookmaking. Second, his phone records show quite a few calls to your client's office, as well as numerous calls to a certain individual in Gardena, who is a known bookmaker.

"We pulled your client's phone records, and see that there are numerous calls to Mister Flange's telephone number, and also the same number of calls to a telephone in New Jersey. The east coast telephone number is registered to a man who lives in a small apartment near the Newark Airport, and for some strange reason, he has six telephones there, which leads us to believe that he is also involved in illegal bookmaking.

"The main difference between the bookmaker in New Jersey and Mister Flange out here, is that

187

Mister Flange neglected to pay his 'union' dues, and was therefore in violation of the illegal gambling industry's regulations.

"Ordinarily, most of the bookmaking offenses are only misdemeanors, as far as the legal system is concerned, but the illegal gambling industry has a different set of rules. Let's just say that their punishment for violations is a little harsher than ours.

"The way it looks to us, your client has been making quite a few bets with both of these bookmakers, probably playing them against each other by arbitraging the odds, and that's not a nice thing to do. In fact, because he was using the telephone and U.S. Mail, we tend to frown upon his actions."

I don't like the way this conversation is going. Snell can't do anything to Stuart on the murder case, but he might try to force Stuart to testify against the New Jersey bookmaker, and that might cause injuries not covered by Stuart's Blue Cross.

"Snell, why don't you have your assistant escort Mister Schwarzman out to his car and let him go home to rest? You and I can finish this conversation after he's gone.

Snell looks at me for almost a full minute, and I can almost hear the gears spinning in his brain. He then tells his assistant what both Stuart and I want to hear: "Please help Mister Schwarzman outside to his car. He's free to leave, and I don't think we'll have any further need for his assistance."

Stuart looks like a guy who just got a reprieve two seconds before they were ready to pull the switch. Some color comes back into his face and he follows Snell's assistant out the door. He looks back at me with a tremendous look of relief on his face. I hope he knows that the meter is still running. Once the door closes behind Stuart, Snell looks at me with an expression that lets me know it's my move.

"I know you've got better things to do than chase after bookmakers, and the police are hungrily waiting for you to give them this homicide case back, so why don't we get right to the commercial here?

"In your infinite wisdom, you agreed to let my client walk, so it's time for me to pay my dues. You're still interested in the film piracy operation aren't you? Okay, I'll take your silence as consent, so here's what I'm going to do. One of my other clients is charged with murder, and because he's a twenty-year police veteran, a group of his friends have been doing a thorough investigation into anyone who might lead them to who the real killer is.

"These guys are not interested in film piracy. All they want to do is find a killer and clear their friend, so the information they get, including photos of the film piracy gang, is of no use to them.

"We haven't finished sorting out all the details yet, but we have a pretty good idea of who did the killing, and it looks like it all centered around control of the piracy gang. My client's trial is coming up soon, and if you and your gang want to show up there, I think that there may be a present waiting for you."

This gets his attention.

"Are you telling me that you'll be turning the piracy gang over to me on the day of your client's trial?"

"That's the way it looks. But don't worry, I'll give you some leads in advance, so that when you make the bust, you can legitimately tell the press that you've been investigating the case for a while and knew that the conspirators would all be in the courtroom during this trial. It'll be just like the last time. You'll make the bust, and get all the credit."

"What kind of clues can you give me now?"

"I can tell you the address that the operation works out of, but we still don't have the final proof of who did the killing we're interested in. I'll give you some information, but you'll have to give me your word that you won't barge in and screw up our investigation just to get some advance publicity. This gang is operating all over the world, and we're still in the process of following the money trail. Also, there's a possibility that the people we're looking at are only the laborers, with some higher-ups actually calling the shots.

"If you can just work on the part of the case that I ask you to, and use the tools at your disposal to find out things that we have no way of learning, then I think there'll be a happy ending to both of our cases."

"Okay, Sharp, where do you suggest we start?"

This meeting is a success. Not only is Stuart off the hook, but I've also got Snell talked into working for us. The one thing his guys can do that our guys can't, is access income tax returns, bank records, and other information that we would never be able to get a subpoena for. One of Tony's investigators got the license number off a truck that made an evening delivery to the Venice Soundstage. This was obviously a load of blank VD stock that

Renaldo needed for production of the pirated copies. I ask Snell to run the plates and get a copy of that truck's recent dispatch records, to see how much blank recording stock has been delivered to Renaldo, when the deliveries were made, and how they were paid for.

The odds are strongly against Renaldo and his people reporting the income from their pirated copies. Knowing how many copies they ran, along with the knowledge that each one brought in at least twenty dollars of profit, can lead to the forming of an educated estimate of how much income they hid, and didn't report to the IRS. This alone would give Snell grounds for an arrest. During the days of prohibition, a gangster named Al Capone did a lot of things, including murder. When he was finally arrested and sent to jail, it was on the only thing that they could definitely prove against him: avoiding paying income tax.

My suggestion to count the blank recording stock delivered to Renaldo isn't a new one. For many years IRS auditors have estimated the volume of business that houses of prostitution have conducted by a similar method: they would count the number of towels sent in each week to the laundry service, presuming that each towel represented one 'trick.'

As I pull out of the Federal Building's parking lot, I hear a car horn tooting. In my rear view mirror I see that it's Stuart. I pick up my cell phone and call him, letting him know that I'm going to the Charthouse for an early dinner, and now that he's a completely free man above suspicion, he will be allowed to pick up my dinner check.

Stuart is all ears and won't be satisfied until he hears a complete report of the conversation I had with Snell, after he left the room. I can appreciate his anxiety, especially after he sat in his car for a half hour, waiting for me to leave the Federal Building. I don't want to go into details about the piracy operation, so I politely tell Stuart that the only way to get him off of the hook on the gambling thing was to give Snell some information on another federal crime that was accidentally uncovered during our investigation of Tony's murder case.

All that Stuart is really interested in is my assurance that he has absolutely nothing to worry about concerning his now-defunct gambling operation. The thing that was most surprising was how that scam had grown. Now that it's all over, Stuart confides in me that his interests also included football and basketball games in which competing bookmakers would offer different point spreads and make it easier to place bets, or 'get down' locally, without worrying about money traveling from coast to coast.

I tell Stuart that if he really wants to leave the gambling business with a clean slate, he should calculate exactly how much he won over the entire period of time he was gambling, and be sure to declare the extra income on his next tax report. I think he finally realizes that the only way to get out clean with no future liability is to do it my way. I tell him that all he has to do is claim that he won it in one weekend trip to Las Vegas. The IRS won't argue with him. They'll be glad to accept his tax money.

After dinner I take a leisurely walk back to the boat, mentally calculating how many hours I can bill Stuart for. Let's see… he called me before one in the afternoon, and it's now a little after five. I guess that four hours at one-fifty each would be fair. The thing I really like about this six hundred that'll be coming in is that the kid has no way of glomming onto it and turning it into a 'firm' fee.

Back at the boat, I see that there are a couple of garbage bags waiting to be taken out. There are one or two chores that have been assigned to me, so in addition to lugging huge bags of dog food from her electric cart onto the boat, taking out the garbage is the other. There are a couple of attractive Rubbermaid trash containers that are placed near each one of the boat docks. Unfortunately, they open from the top, and the kid can't reach high enough to open them. She's already got the dog trained to stand on his rear legs, use a paw to pull open a mailbox door, and drop mail from his mouth down into the mailbox. If she can get him to do that, I don't see why she can't get him to take out the garbage too.

While dumping the 'recyclable' bag, I notice some empty envelopes from the IRS, several major movie studios, and the Motion Picture Association. As usual, I have absolutely no idea of what's going on, but I hope it has something to do with us finding the real killer because at this point, I still have no defense for Tony's murder case that can be supported by any evidence. It's still all just a theory

A popular television courtroom drama utilized what the actors called their 'plan B,' which consisted of directing guilt away from their own client and trying to get the jury to believe that another person may have committed the crime their client was charged with. It would be nice if we could bring up all the film piracy stuff at Tony's trial and get the jury to think that someone in Renaldo's gang killed Joe for stumbling onto the criminal enterprise. Unfortunately, in real life, you can't get away with that. In order to bring in evidence of completely unrelated crimes and start finger pointing in other directions, you must have some shred of evidence that the direction you're going in is actually true, and not just a theory. Now all I've got is my theory that Renaldo had Joe killed to get him out of the way and stop him from going to the authorities.

Whenever I think about blaming someone for a crime I always like to see what possible defense they could come up with, and in this case I'm afraid that Renaldo would walk away with an acquittal, because he was at work when the murder was committed, and there's nothing we have to connect him with anyone who's a likely shooter.

In addition to our problems with Tony's case, the kid is in an especially bad mood because not only has her good friend Myra subpoenaed her as a witness, but Suzi was told that she couldn't bring the dog to court with her. I don't know what bothers her most - being subpoenaed or not being able to bring the dog.

On a previous case we worked on, the kid managed to bring her dog into the courtroom by using a devious deception, and only got away with it because officially, the court wasn't in session at the time. I hope she doesn't try another trick like that this time.

Tony's investigation teams are still covering the Venice Soundstage from dusk to dawn, and a new report has come in about another truck delivery. The alley surveillance guys counted two cartons being unloaded from the truck. They then followed the truck back to its garage in Chatsworth, where it pulled into a large warehouse.

Following up on the warehouse information, we've learned that the place is a major distributor of blank DVD stock to duplicators, and that their main product is a 4.7 gigabyte DVD that gets packed one hundred to a box, and ten boxes to a case. If the truck left two cases, that means Renaldo ordered two thousand pieces. Further investigation of the distributor revealed that they make at least two deliveries there every month.

This is looking bigger than I thought, because if Renaldo is running off four thousand copies a month, it means the gang may be taking in as much as three quarters of a million dollars each month, and that's enough to be a good motive for murder.

Tony says that when he got the phone call to meet Joe that evening, it was just as he was stepping aboard his boat. This means that his answering machine answered the call, and Tony shut it off when he started talking to the caller. Fortunately, the portion of the tape that had that call on it hasn't been taped over yet, so we play it back. All it contains is a voice that says "Tony? If you're there, please pick up. I'm calling for Joe, at the soundstage..." At that point, Tony had reached the phone, picked up the handset, and the answering machine automatically stopped recording.

Suzi takes the answering machine tape, hooks it up to her computer's audio input, and digitizes the few words that the caller said before Tony picked up the phone. Using some of the sophisticated software bought from Mister Necktie, she now has a voiceprint of the caller.

Being professional investigators, each one of Tony's crew recorded their interviews with the film company employees, including everyone on the set, from production assistants up to Will Sargent, the guy who took over Joe's job. Suzi takes all of the cassettes and digitizes them, hoping to get a voiceprint comparison, because during the interviews, no one admitted to having made the call summoning Tony to that evening meeting with Joe.

This job will take the kid a day or so to complete, so at this point we've still got nothing other than the knowledge that Renaldo's operation is much bigger than I thought it was.

The phone rings. It's Snell calling. He doesn't waste any time with small talk.

"Our investigation has reached a point where we're ready to make some arrests. We followed through on your leads, and the distribution company sold thousands of blank DVD's to the gang, but that wasn't all: they also provided them with a DVD duplication system, complete with a deck for playing the DVCAM master, three distribution amps, all the necessary cables, switchers, monitors, and forty-five high quality DVD burners, all equipped with automatic loading devices and disc printing software. All one has to do is load the master, put blank DVD's in the autoloaders, press a button, and leave the equipment alone. The system's burners are capable of turning out 90 DVD's every hour. If he let them go all night long, the next morning there could be almost a thousand copies waiting for him. All he then has to do is slip them into the black cases, and they're ready to be packaged and mailed out.

"If you want to us to hold off with our arrests, then we'd like you to make our job easier by assuring us that per your promise, all the players will be in court on the same day."

I was curious about who else was involved, particularly Evelyn. If she wasn't getting any money, then I'll know that it was her daughter that was doing the evening mailings. I press Snell for whatever I could get out of him.

"What about the money? Did you get any bank info? You must have gotten something, or you wouldn't be ready to make the arrests."

Snell is the ultimate professional FBI guy. Even when you're on his side, you can't get him to talk.

"I can't tell you most of the details, but suffice it to say that the distribution company's bills were paid by direct bank transfer from an offshore account. The same foreign bank makes pay-online transfers each month to pay off the credit card bills of the gang's three main players. A lady named Evelyn, her daughter, and that Renaldo fellow. Other than that, no one else gets any money... now. However, in the past six months that they were operating, the largest share went to your murder victim.

"Now, can we trust that you'll have all the players in court for us?"

I'm crushed. Not only is the new love of my life a criminal, my entire theory has also just collapsed. I felt sure that Joe Caulfield was an innocent guy who just happened to stumble onto a film piracy scheme. Now it looks like I was wrong about him. He was a major player. Thinking back, it all seems to fit. Not only was he running the piracy operation of the few films that Renaldo could bring home from the theater, he was planning the creation of a film courier service that would give him access to all of the big studio releases.

Trying hard enough, it still might be possible for unhappiness with Joe's getting a majority share of the profits to be a motive for his murder, but it wouldn't make any sense for them to kill off the guy who was trying to help them get their hands on blockbuster releases from the big studios.

This also means that we're back to square one, with no motive for Joe's murder, and no suspects. If things keep going like this, I'll have no defense at Tony's trial other than trying to implicate Renaldo's gang, and it's not likely that the D.A. will allow me to get that into evidence. I'm starting to feel that sinking feeling that I only get when I have a losing case, no defense, but a client that I feel is innocent.

Our only hope now is that the kid can come up with a voiceprint match. That might lead us to the killer.

The phone rings and I see that it's Evelyn calling. This is terrible. Not only do I now know that she's a crook, but I have to also look at her as a possible murder suspect. Reluctantly, I pick up the phone.

"Hi, sailor, it's your long lost friend Evelyn."

198

"Hello, beautiful, I was just thinking about you."

"Really?"

"Yes. As a matter of fact, I was going to call you."

"Does this mean I'm going to get to see you again?"

"In a way, yes. I've been pretty busy with this murder case, but I think we've finally got it solved."

"Really. Who did it? I'm dying to know."

"Well, that's privileged information as of now, but I can tell you that the cops working on the case have someone, and I've been informed that an arrest may be made soon. I just hope it's before the trial, because if it isn't, I'll be going to court without any decent defense."

"Well, I sure hope you have better luck getting your man than I've had."

"Hey, I've got a great idea. Tony is inviting some of the film crew to watch the last day of the trial, when I do my brilliant summation. Why don't you and your daughter join them? You know that I've got some connections with the D.A.'s office. If you want to come, I can arrange for you to have front row seats. Tony will be inviting Renaldo there too, so there'll be plenty of familiar faces there for your daughter to have a reunion with."

I feel terrible doing this, knowing that Snell and his gang will be arresting her that day. Maybe I can talk him into waiting until I've left the courtroom before he makes the bust. In a way, I hope she declines my invitation.

"Oh Peter, that would be great. Are you sure you can get us seats?"

199

14

I must be the biggest louse in town. I know that Evelyn and her daughter will be arrested, and I've just invited her right into Snell's trap. Tony will be calling Renaldo to invite him to be there too, so now it's up to me to arrange for the seating.

From what I've seen and heard, the press will be there in full force. It's not very often that you see a twenty-year police veteran with several valor awards go to trial on a murder charge. I've got a pretty good reputation for pulling things out of the hat at the last minute of a trial, but my trick bag is empty this time. If the kid doesn't come up with a voiceprint match I've got no defense at all, other than a weak contention that there's no way the prosecution can tell when that empty bullet shell became empty.

I dial Myra's private line. She's in the office.

"Hello Peter, are you calling to talk about a plea? My offer of Man One won't be on the table after they swear in the jury."

"I'm sorry to disappoint you my dear, but this is not a plea bargain call. I need a little favor that has nothing to do with the case, directly."

"What could you possibly want?"

"I need three front row seats in the peanut gallery."

"Okay, Petey, let's have it. I know something's going on, and I want to know what it is."

"There's nothing going on. I want to invite some people to the last day of the trial, and because the press is having a feeding frenzy, I thought you might help me out here."

"No sale, Pete. I've already received a similar call from Special Agent Snell's office. The FBI has also requested several seats. It's just too coincidental that both you and Snell want extra seats to the same show. We all hate coincidences, so let's have it. What are you cooking up? Another one of your famous courtroom spectaculars? I have a right to know about it."

"I'll make you a promise. You get those extra seats for me, and let Snell and his boys come in too, and whatever happens, I'll make sure that you wind up being a hero. You know I've done it in the past, and that's why you're sitting in that office up there. I'm not running for office, so I don't need any free publicity. Snell's going to get his, and if you talk nice to him, I'm sure he'll share the spotlight with you - especially when you call him back after we hang up, and make it a condition of his getting seats inside the courtroom, instead of out in the hall."

She hesitates for a while.

"Are you sure this extravaganza you're planning won't upset my applecart?"

"Myra, I give you my word that the sideshow Snell and I are planning have absolutely nothing to do with your murder case. And, in the event that we also happen to get lucky and nail the actual shooter, causing your case to tank, then I'll see to it that you also get credit for nailing the new perp too."

She sounds afraid of what we've got planned.

"Is this going to be like the last time? When the whole courtroom was a madhouse? I don't want to see that happen again."

"Not exactly. We won't be riding to court in a limo this time."

"You know what I mean, Peter. Will it be another circus?"

"I hope not, but if it does happen, it'll be your fault."

"My fault? How can you say that? What did I do?"

"Two bad things. First, you arrested and charged an innocent man. But that's not the big mistake you made."

"Oh yeah? What's the big one, smart guy?"

"You subpoenaed the kid to testify, and told her she can't bring her dog to court."

"C'mon Pete, you know I can't allow a dog in the courtroom. And we've already discussed why she had to be subpoenaed. It's because of her fingerprints on that shell casing."

"Yes I know, but that doesn't make any difference. The deed has been done, and I wouldn't want to be in the shoes of anyone who that kid is mad at, no matter how legitimate your reasons were."

Myra tells me that she has a feeling of what I mean. She and the kid share a mutual love and admiration for each other, but Myra did a bad thing and the kid is going to see that Myra gets spanked for it. I can't wait to see what the kid has planned. Myra probably can't either, because she says she'll be sitting in the back row watching.

Tony left a message for me that Renaldo has been invited to the trial, and he'll be there in the front row. The cast of characters is almost complete. Now all that remains is for me to figure out some legal defense for Tony - one that has a chance of actually working.

It may be starting. I just saw an email come into the office in answer to our request to have an independent ballistic expert examine the empty shell casing. This is particularly interesting, because I'm the attorney of record on Tony's case, and I never made any request like this.

Every once in a while the kid takes over the controls, and I'm made to feel like I'm just along for the ride, with her doing the driving. For some strange reason I'm starting to get that feeling again. I'm tempted to ask her about it, but she's not on the boat. I see her electric cart parked near the boats, but there's no sign of her on the boat. The dog's gone too. No surprise there.

On my way to the Marina Liquor Store I pass by Tony's sailboat and see the dog sleeping guard on his aft deck. This means the kid is in there. Tony's not here, and looking in the boat, I can't see the kid, but that's no surprise because she's not tall enough to be seen from outside the boat. There's plenty of activity going on, because the Asian Boys are loading supplies onto the boat. I hope that Tony isn't planning to skip out on us.

Returning from the liquor store, I see that the dog is no longer on Tony's boat, so the dynamic duo is probably back on our boat. There's a manila envelope waiting for me that looks like it's from Jack B. that is probably his report on the owners of April's apartment building. This would be good time to sit back, have a beer or two, or three, and read Jack's report.

There's a knock at the hull. It's not Mister Necktie this time, but a guy wearing a leather apron. I've never seen him before.

"Yes sir, can I help you?"

"I'm the shoemaker."

"So?"

"I have an appointment to measure Mister Bernie."

Why not? This should be no surprise to me. In addition to us being the best-equipped forensic science boat in the Marina, the dog will now have some custom made shoes to wear. I'd like to see how she justifies using the firm's money for this project. Another remarkable fact is that the dog now has a title. Not only do we have 'Doctor Braunstien,' we also have 'Mister Bernie.' I wonder what my official title is. No, I know what it is: 'Big human who does heavy lifting.'

I invite the shoemaker aboard, sit back, pop open a beer, and start reading Jack's report. I can't seem to concentrate on the report. For some reason, the shoemaker and Bernie are in the main saloon with me, and Bernie is getting measured... but not for shoes. Instead, Mister Leather Apron is measuring him for what looks like a special harness or something. I remember the last time the kid finagled this dog into court, and I hope that this isn't part of another grand scheme of hers.

The shoemaker has finished his measuring session and is now leaving the boat. Jack's report now has my full attention. As he mentioned to me in the past, the apartment building that April lives in is owned by a real estate trust controlled by Chad and

Ruth Sinclair. The bulk of this report concentrates on their unique lifestyle and beliefs.

The Sinclairs have received quite a bit of press coverage over the years because of their creation and leadership of an infamous right-wing white supremist militia group out near Lancaster, California, the farthest northeast portion of Los Angeles County, about forty miles from the San Fernando Valley.

Sinclairs themselves haven't committed any crimes, but their followers have certainly had some well publicized brushes with the law. Some characteristics that most of these extremist groups seem to share are hatred and distrust of government, hatred of anyone but white people, a hatred of and refusal to pay income tax, and a belief that the laws of this country don't apply to them.

The exploits of some of them have become very well known. A woman claimed that the United States Government owed her many millions of dollars, for defrauding her into thinking that she should pay income tax. She conducted her own court, found the government liable, issued a judgment, and then sold portions of the judgment to gullible believers, in the form of legal-looking certificates that resembled diplomas from Harvard. One elderly couple I know were so taken in by her baloney, that they bought a 'certificate' from her that was supposed to be worth over sixty thousand dollars. I understand that she was selling them for less than ten cents on the dollar. The elderly couple tried to pay off their mortgage with her phony certificate, and ultimately wound up losing their home.

Other believers had refused to file income tax returns, and many have been sent to Federal Prison. The most notable in that group includes Mister Irwin Schiff, who authored most of his anti-tax manuals while a guest at the U.S. Government's 'greybar hotel'. Whenever he's in between prison sentences, he usually makes the talk show rounds.

The more mundane followers fall into groups that include skinheads and other terribly misguided, armed people, who participate in Al Qaeda-like training, in preparation for some eventual government takeover, during which time all their guns will be confiscated. One member of this group was the late Timothy McVeigh, who showed his utter disregard for others in Oklahoma, when he blew up the Alfred P. Murrah Federal Building on April 9, 1995, killing 168 people. He was ultimately put to death by lethal injection, but not after the government that he so hated spent millions of dollars helping him get a fair trial.

Another of their ilk is the highly decorated war hero Colonel James 'Bo' Gritz, who ran for President of the United States in 1992. He first drew attention as the ex-Green Beret who led the Ross Perot-financed commando-style missions into Southeast Asia, to rescue POW's he believed to have been imprisoned since the Vietnam War. Many people believe that because James Bo Gritz's nickname was 'Jambo,' Sylvester Stallone created the Rambo character in his image - especially in the movies that shared Gritz's beliefs with respect to American prisoners of war.

Gritz's manifesto brought out into the light of day what most of his like-minded followers believed in - an end to foreign aid, an end to the federal income tax, dismantling of the Federal Reserve System, absolutely no gun control, and a recognition that the United States of America is a 'White Christian Nation.'

The beliefs of people like McVeigh and the Sinclairs were eloquently stated once by Gritz in a comment he made during the 2000 Presidential contest between George W. Bush and Al Gore: "...Jews, feminists, sodomites and other liberal activists may install Gore over an apathetic moral majority...runaway abortion, anti-Christ/God and globalism are certain."

Well, at least I now have an idea what we're dealing with here. I'd like to see the looks on their faces if the Sinclairs were around whenever April's boyfriend of color visited. The Sinclairs are also champions of what has been referred to as a 'sovereign state citizen' movement, whereby the believers disclaim their United States citizenship in a misguided attempt to exempt themselves from all of the laws that the rest of us mere citizens are compelled to obey. These people have gone so far as to assert their believed status as a defense to everything from non-payment of income tax, to driving without a driver's license, contending that the Courts have no jurisdiction over them. That goes over big with the judges; that's why so many of them write their books in cells.

The Sinclairs probably don't believe in the terms of a written apartment lease either, unless they're completely unaware of what their manager Miller is doing to April, and who knows how many other tenants.

I'm glad Jack did such a thorough report on these people because it certainly shows me a side of society that I wasn't that familiar with. Unfortunately though, it doesn't give me anything that will help with Tony's defense - but then again, it wasn't supposed to. And thinking of April, I never had a chance to watch those commercials of Hershel's that I recorded, so I might as well see what they look like. I programmed the machine to record a commercial each nite, during the second break of the late movie.

Looking at the commercials this way is strange because each time I see April she looks a little thinner. At one time she mentioned that her boyfriend Joe didn't want her to lose weight, but now that he's gone, she must have decided to start a diet. I can't wait to see her in a couple of months to find out what the girl inside really looks like.

As I walk down the dock, Tony motions for me to come aboard his boat. He gives me a report on the investigations his team is still conducting. I don't want to burst his balloon, but I still don't see any defense tactic to use. Without his .50 caliber gun, he has no desire to visit the firing range, so he spends all of his time working on the case.

I also notice some things missing from his boat, mainly the equipment that he and Suzi used to reload his shell casings. The workbench is also empty, with all the empty shells gone. Tony tells me all that stuff was picked up by some company that does computer analysis of those things. It looks like the stress is finally getting to him, because he must have lost at least another ten pounds in the past couple of weeks.

Considering the large recent expenditure that our law firm just made in computer software, I'm curious to know why all of his reloading equipment was sent out to another company. Is it possible for someone else to have more stuff than the kid? I make a mental note to inquire, but then realize that it would be an effort in futility.

Back at the boat, the phone is ringing. It's Myra calling.

"Hello beautiful. Calling for a date?"

"You know what she did?"

"By she, I assume you mean the adorable little girl that we both know and love. Right?"

"That little brat is demanding that we stipulate to the fact that she can testify as an expert witness in ballistic fingerprinting. How can she expect that? She's not even a teenager yet. She can't possibly…"

"Okay, okay, just calm down. You know she's still mad at you for subpoenaing just her, without also including the dog. What harm can she do? If you really believe that she doesn't have that much knowledge on the subject, then it doesn't make any difference. In fact you'd be doing yourself a favor by stipulating. That way her qualifications or lack thereof don't get in front of the jury, and all it means is that she'll be able to offer an opinion in her testimony.

"Remember, you're the one who wants her there, so why not let her have the spotlight for a few minutes? I think she's been rehearsing her lines for the past day or so, and probably thinks she'll be holding a press conference after the trial. C'mon, she's just a kid. Let her have her way this time. We both know that when this trial is over, you'll both be talking on the phone every day, like nothing ever happened."

"Maybe you're right. I hope this doesn't come back to bite me in the ass."

Fortunately, the conversation ends before I have too much time to concentrate on her ass. From what I now know, I think Myra should get some ass-bite medicine. It would be a very bad idea for her to get on the wrong side of this kid. Obviously Myra has no idea about Tony's equipment having been sent out for examination, because she didn't mention receiving any notice of additional witnesses being added to our list.

Any thoughts I may have had about asking the kid what's going on also bring to my attention that the doctor and Mister Bernie are not on the boat. I look out the window and see that her electric cart is still parked, but there's no sign of her. I call her cell phone.

"Yes, what is it?"

"I see that you and your assistant aren't on the boat and your e-cart is still here. Are you very far away?"

"I'm in Santa Monica, on business."

"You haven't taken my Hummer, have you?"

"No. I have a driver today. Dinner will be brought over at seven this evening. Please be on time."

No information, no answers, just a command to be on time for dinner. She said that it would be 'brought over,' which means that the Asian Boys will be delivering and serving us another gourmet meal. At first I was under the impression that all they would ever be bringing to the boat is Chinese food, but I was wrong. On different occasions they've been known to deliver goodies from other places in the Marina, like the Cheesecake Factory, and Jerry's Deli.

I may not know what's always going on around here, but at least the food is good.

Any question I might have had as to who her driver is gets answered when I see Stuart carrying a box to the boat. When he unpacks it for placement in the forward stateroom, I see that it's the ammunition reloading equipment and Tony's supply of empty cartridges, which he meticulously counts and brings home after each trip to the firing range.

During dinner, Stuart assures me that his gambling days are behind him, and that all of his other legitimate enterprises are coming along nicely. He also mentions that I may be seeing him on television in the near future, because he's thinking of doing some commercials for one of his products.

Of course no dinner with Stuart is complete without him telling me about a new business he's thinking of putting together, and tonight is no exception. This time, it's a completely online venture with no warehouse space or inventory required. Stuart became intrigued with some statistics he heard during one of his law lectures and is concerned that there are too many people out there who've never made out a Last Will and Testament. His plan is to create a new national Will Registry, where anyone in the country can use his service to file a Will. He then plans to notify every funeral parlor in the country about the service, so that whenever a deceased is brought in, their statistics are fed into his Registry to see if there is a Will on file there.

If a person doesn't have a Will prepared, Stuart will offer several sample templates with numerous paragraphs that can be selected and edited online, to be cut and pasted into a final document. There will be a nominal fee charged, in the neighborhood of about twenty or thirty dollars, and Stuart feels that in no time at all, he should have several million people in the Registry.

In addition to serving private individuals, he intends to offer a reduced rate to Attorneys and Trust Departments of banks, so that they will list their clients' names and statistics with him. The wholesale division catering to professionals will not require actual storage of the text of those Wills, and instead only contain the fact that a Will does exist, and who the custodian is. As an extra incentive to get lawyers to sign up and register their clients' Will locations, Stuart will be adding their names to his national list of Will preparers, so that visitors to his site can find the nearest attorney by zip code.

I've got to hand it to Stuart. He comes up with quite a few hair-brained schemes, but every once in while, he gets lucky with something that actually can be of use to a great number of people. This time, I think he's got a keeper.

The pleasant dinner concludes. As usual, Suzi just sat and listened all evening. I have a feeling that the computer in her brain has stored every word she's heard every person say for the past ten years.

The kid must have been busy last night after dinner, because my phone is ringing and I see Myra's number displayed. I can usually tell what mood she's in by how many seconds of greeting time I'm allowed. Today it's down to zero, so the mood can't be too good.

"Peter, what the hell's going on with Tony's murder case?"

"I'm just fine thank you, how about yourself?"

"Please, spare me. I want to know what type of show you plan on putting on next week at his trial."

"Myra, is there something I've done since our last conversation that's prompted you to make this call to me?"

"No Peter, you haven't done anything... it's her."

"By her, I assume you mean the little witness you pissed off by subpoenaing without including her companion?"

"Yes, that's exactly who I mean. When I got into the office this morning there was an email from her instructing me to tell my trial deputy not to make a relevancy objection to the questions you ask one of our witnesses."

"What witness would that be, pray tell?"

"She wouldn't say, but I think it might be her. I explained to her that if you wanted to ask her questions beyond the scope of our direct examination, that you could call her as your own witness."

She's right. Something is definitely going on, but as usual, I haven't the slightest idea of what it is. Obviously the kid has some information that I'm supposed to bring it out in cross-examination.

"Myra, I know you'll believe me when I tell you that little Doctor Braunstien hasn't told me anything about this line of questioning yet, but I'm sure she'll give me instructions before we get to the trial. I'll tell you what - as soon as I know what the heck is going on, I'll give you a heads-up, so that you can prepare your trial deputy."

That seems to have satisfied her for now. I'm getting the feeling that Renaldo is in for a heap of trouble. I had a hunch that the prosecution would be calling some witnesses to establish Tony's motive, but I didn't know that Renaldo would be one of them. I hope this doesn't screw up Special Agent Snell's arrest plans, because I'm sure he's planning on taking Renaldo, Evelyn, and her daughter into custody after the trial.

The reporters are in their usual feeding-frenzy mode as Tony's trial date approaches. Every time you see a local newscast, some blow-dried bimbo is standing in front of the Venice Soundstage with a 'new breaking development' in the murder case, which usually consists of a neighbor down the street saying that they really didn't hear any gunshot, so the soundstage must be soundproofed.

Our office is not making any statements about what tactics we'll use in Tony's defense. I keep watching the news, hoping they'll interview one of the legal geniuses they have on stand-by. Maybe the legal eagle will say something like 'well, if I was trying this case, here's the type of defense I'd put on...' I sure can use all the help I can get, because at this point it looks like Tony had better be instructed to bring a toothbrush with him to the trial. He might not be going home after it's over.

If nothing new turns up that can help me clear Tony, I'm going to have to call an office meeting and ask the kid for some help. She got me into this mess, so maybe she can figure out some way for me to get out of it.

I don't see the cops hanging around Tony's boat that much, so their investigations have probably hit dead-ends too. There's plenty of action around his motorsailer, but it's not for the case, it's the Asian Boys getting it all ready for a cruise. Maybe I should tell him to take it before the trial, while he still has a chance.

There's a knock at the hull. Looking over the side I see a familiar face. It's Vaughn, an explosives expert we used on a case not too long ago when some vehicles were being blown up. He's a former FBI lab tech who retired and went out on his own and now consults with various law enforcement agencies on anything that has to do with a bang.

"Hello Vaughn, come on aboard. To what do I owe this pleasure today?"

"Hello Peter. It's nice to see you too, but to tell the truth, I'm here because Suzi called me in for a consult. I'm sure you know what it's all about, right?"

"Well, I like to leave all the minor details of the cases to her. I just do the big things, like going into court and making a fool out of myself. She's in her stateroom. Her assistant is coming out now to escort you in there."

Vaughn follows the dog and disappears into the forensic laboratory formerly known as the foreward stateroom. Aside from the explosion that someone's .50 caliber gun made when Joe got shot, I don't know about any other explosions that Vaughn could consult with her about.

It's now the night before Tony's trial is scheduled and I can't sleep a wink. I hate this feeling. It's not butterflies about going to trial that are getting to me, it's the dread of certain failure. Tony's not a close friend of mine, but he's still a client, and he's depending on me to represent him to the best of my ability. Ordinarily I wouldn't be worried, but this time is different. I didn't pick this case, it was dumped in my lap, and it's a dead-bang loser.

The prosecution has the smoking gun, complete with spent shell casing. The defendant had the means, motive, and opportunity. After Myra gets a successful conviction, I wouldn't be surprised if District Attorneys all around the country use a transcript of this trial as a textbook example of how to win a case.

My career won't suffer too much, because everyone already believes Tony is guilty, so they'll respect me for trying to do my best on his behalf. My career isn't what's in danger. It's my ego. I really don't like to lose. And to make matters worse, they're going to use the kid against me.

I've gone over the case hundreds of times in my mind and other than the film pirates, the only thing that I can possibly use to create some reasonable doubt is that empty shell casing, and how ridiculous it is to believe that an experienced detective like Tony would leave it in his weapon's cylinder and then call the cops to the scene. If I can get them to believe that it may have been planted in his gun by someone else then I've got a slim chance of getting at least one of the jurors on our side who will vote for an acquittal.

But even if the jury hangs up with no decision, Myra will probably re-file the case and try him over again, so all I'd be doing is creating another chance to lose. This is not a good situation. I can't remember ever going to trial before with less of a defense to offer.

As long as I'm awake, I might as well watch some late night television and see how April and Hershel are doing. The movie is an old black-and-white one featuring Edward G. Robinson as a bad guy. When the commercial break comes up I see Hershel riding on a Segway scooter from car to car on his trade-in lot. Then, as usual, April slowly rides by him in a convertible, but it's a full-sized one, and not the little one she used in her first commercial.

The next thing Hershel does really takes me by surprise. He asks April to stop her car and step out of it. When she does, I can see a noticeable weight loss. She lifts up her arms, proudly rotates for the camera, then gets back into the convertible and drives out of the picture.

Hershel is now holding up some container and talking about how April decided to go on a diet, and the stuff he's holding up is the product she's using. He goes on to say that he didn't ask her to lose weight, but she insisted on doing it anyway, and he was so impressed with the stuff she's using that he decided to become a main distributor.

As Hershel talks more about the stuff and how you can order it through his dealership, a close-up of the container appears on the screen and I see that it's Stuart's weight-loss snake oil. Hershel goes on and on about how wonderful it is, and that when used in conjunction with a suggested plan of reducing caloric intake and regular exercise, it can work for you too. Well duh. Even a glass of water will make you lose weight if you combine it with diet and exercise.

He goes so far as to offer a free case of the stuff with the purchase of any new or used car from his dealership. Only in America. I press the 'power' button and the screen fades to black.

THE TRIAL

The first day or so of any jury trial is usually taken up with the seating of a jury, during which time each side has a certain amount of chances to bounce prospective jurors that they're not happy with, for one reason or another. In this particular case the prosecution wants to get rid of any juror who has a relative on any police force, for fear that they might sympathize with the defendant. On the other hand, I want to cleanse the jury pool of anyone who feels they've been victimized by a police officer by any means, from a wrongful traffic ticket, bad rap or brutality.

Jury selection is going faster than I've ever seen before, so the judge tells us to be ready for opening statements after the lunch break. I join Tony and several of his investigating team in the courthouse cafeteria. He looks like he's lost about twenty pounds since this mess started, but by the way he's eating, the weight loss didn't come from any loss of appetite.

After lunch Myra's trial deputy presents her opening argument, and it's a textbook statement. She starts out by introducing herself and then goes on to explain the charge against the defendant and how she will introduce evidence to support every element of the crime and the defendant's connection with it. By the time she's finished, she almost has me believing in Tony's guilt. This makes my job even harder because in my opening I not only have to convince the jury that there's reasonable doubt in his guilt, but I also have to talk myself into believing it.

She finishes her opening statement in less than an hour, so there's time for me to get mine in today. I always like to have the jury conclude their day after having heard something good for my client's case. If I time things right, after I finish my opening statement, I'll try to talk the judge into recessing until tomorrow morning. I look around to see if Myra's sitting somewhere in the back, but she's nowhere to be seen. There are a few reporters present, along with the usual amount of trial-watchers. I'm sure the main contingency of bottom feeders are waiting until tomorrow, when the prosecution's evidence starts to come in.

I don't have much of a defense to give them a preview of, so I take the opposite tack by urging them to use their common sense. There's hardly ever a way for prosecutors to make a visual presentation of a defendant actually committing a murder, so these are all circumstantial cases that require the jury to connect the dots in their own minds and come to a conclusion.

In this case, it's the dot-connection process that I want them to concentrate on, because it's just too illogical to expect things to go down the way the prosecution contends. It would require Tony to have the knowledge that the victim would be working late in his office and that the rear door to the soundstage would be open after hours, allowing him to enter. It would also require the luck of having no other people in the entire building.

The prosecution would also have them believe that the defendant, who had been involved in several previous altercations where racism was involved, shot and killed a black man and then without removing the spent cartridge from his weapon, called the police to report the killing.

Not too long ago, a talented journalist named Sebastian Junger wrote a book that was made into a motion picture, coincidentally starring my neighbor. It was entitled *The Perfect Storm*, and depicted a situation at sea wherein every condition possible turned into a storm of perfection. What I'm trying to do in my opening statement is show that with all the evidence that the prosecution has against the defendant, what they're arguing took place is really 'The Perfect Frame,' and that in no way could all the facts pointing to my client's guilt have lined up in such a manner without being arranged by others. This is not an uncontrollable force of nature we're dealing with here, it's a set of man-made circumstances.

I want this jury to see that the odds are so great against the evidence in this case to be laid out in such a perfect way for prosecution, that this must be the result of some devious person who planned the whole affair. I'm trying to liken it to opening up a box that contains a jigsaw puzzle, pouring the pieces out onto a table, and having them fall into place forming the completed puzzle. An occurrence like this isn't impossible, but it's so highly unlikely that I urge them to use their intelligence to find the reasonable doubt that truly exists here.

Tony knows what I'm up against. He doesn't say anything, but I'm sure he knows that what I did with my opening statement was about all that anyone could do.

Before we were sent out for trial, the People estimated that they would need two days to put on their case. They probably never realized that the jury would get seated so quickly, so I would say that they plan on wrapping up their entire case and resting by the lunch break tomorrow. If this is right, then all of the action including the kid's testimony will have to take place tomorrow morning. That works for me, because that's when I've got seats reserved for the three film pirates.

I'm not riding back and forth to court with Tony. He's with his gang, and I've got Jack B. chauffeuring me in the Hummer. Whenever I'm involved in a big case I find that driving can be injurious to my health. In view of the fact that so many traffic accidents are caused by inattention, I don't want to get behind the wheel of this yellow tank while I'm completely pre-occupied with what's going to happen in the courtroom.

I know exactly what's going to happen tomorrow morning, so there probably won't be any surprises awaiting us. It'll probably be a lot like the prelim, only with more explanations, for the jury's sake. They'll do it by the numbers starting with the coroner and then move on to the motive argument and finally the ballistics. About the only thing I'll have any chance of keeping out is several complaints of excessive force against Tony that were made by black people. Police personnel files are usually sealed, especially if the investigations haven't been completed. Tony told me that as of this date there has been no final determination of his misconduct with respect to persons of color, so maybe we can dodge that bullet.

This isn't normal procedure for me, but on the way back to the boat I tell Jack to stop at the Marina del Rey Liquor Store, where I pick up a six-pack of medicine. I intend to sleep tonight, even if it takes the entire container of six doses to get the job done.

It worked. I slept like a baby. No need to worry about a dulling of my senses, because they won't be needed today. The prosecution will put on their case, I'll make a few objections that will be overruled, and then I'll lose. What's got me unnerved most may be the fact that Tony is a calm as he is. He must have nerves of steel, if he has any nerves at all.

As we approach the Santa Monica courthouse I see the press trucks with their satellite dishes extended up in the air, waiting for the juicy news item that a policeman has been convicted of murder. I'm sure they'll be groups of protesters on both side of the issues waiting for their fifteen seconds of fame, when a newscaster desperate for an item to fill some dead air asks them a question about why they're here and waving that sign.

I always wondered about the instantaneous protests I see covered on the news. If they're so instantaneous, where do those nice signs they have come from?

Up ahead is a group of reporters who have spotted my yellow Hummer approaching and they're waiting to ambush me as I walk up from the street to the courthouse entrance. In Santa Monica there's no underground parking lot from which you can sneak in and out. No matter where you park or get dropped off, the press has a good chance to get at you.

From the time that Jack drops me off in front to the time I get to the courthouse door, they shout questions at me. There must be some instruction book that they've read, because their questions follow the same pattern. "Mister Sharp, will your client take the stand today?" "Do you have any alibi witness for your client?" "Are you going to try to blame the crime on someone else?" "Have you negotiated a plea bargain with the D.A.?"

Now that Myra's been elected as District Attorney, there are new questions that they ask me. "Mister Sharp, how does it feel going up against your ex-wife?" Just before I enter the courtroom door and reach the metal-detector, I hear the last question. "Mister Sharp, is it true that your ex-wife is going to use your daughter to testify against your client?"

That's a new one. I hope the kid was watching on television so she can see how her being cute can work to get her friend Tony the death penalty.

Inside the courtroom it looks like a sardine can. They purposely moved this case into the biggest room they have, but it sure doesn't look that big with all these people packed in here. Renaldo is here with Evelyn and her daughter and those two women look great. What a shame they're not going home tonight. And what an interesting seating arrangement there is here. The piracy gang is completely surrounded by Snell and his men.

The first few rows of the spectator seats are full of representatives from quite a few news organizations. Because of past cases in our County with police being charged with crimes, the press is always looking for another Rodney King type of case to help sell their newspapers for the next month.

The judge made a decision to allow one Court TV camera cover the trial, but because it's mounted on a moveable platform controlled remotely, one camera is all they'll need. They can swing the camera around to see everything but the jurors. Neither side objected to the camera coverage. Myra wants the publicity for her office, and I couldn't care less one way or the other. There's going to be no way to hide my loss this time, so they might as well televise it as a perfect negative example for future lawyers to see how not to conduct a trial.

There's an empty seat in the back of the room that one of the bailiffs is guarding, probably for Myra to sit in when she gets here. Her chief trial deputy is an experienced woman who has handled many major cases here, but she doesn't attract the press attention that I do, because she wasn't married to the District Attorney. And, she doesn't' have a 'daughter' testifying against her case today.

Tony managed to have the bailiff save some seats for the members of his team. I've also been told that more cops will be coming later, including some top brass in the department. There's a lot riding on this trial other than Tony's fate, and local law enforcement agencies are all concerned about their images with the public. They've had some serious hits in the recent past, and they aren't looking forward to another one. I guess they want to see the loss with their own eyes, so when it comes time to face the reporters they can say that they were there during the trial, and comment on it intelligently.

As expected, the prosecution starts with the medical examiner. He testifies as to the cause of death. They arrested Tony at about eight-fifteen that evening, and know from his own statement that he arrived at the soundstage twenty minutes earlier, so it wasn't too much of a stretch to expect the coroner to put the time of death at around eight PM.

On cross-examination, the only thing I can do is to try and push my perfect frame theory ahead, so I ask him if it was possible for the time of death to have been one hour earlier. Grudgingly, he finally admits that time of death is always a tough thing to pin down exactly, but yes, the murder could have possibly taken place an hour before Tony got there. Fine. That's all I need from this guy, so I let him go and the D.A. doesn't have any further questions for him on re-direct.

At least I've got the first part of the perfect frame in place. It is possible that the murder took place before Tony got there. Because possibilities are the only things I have to work with in this case, I'm happy to have the first one in place.

After the coroner, they play the recording of Tony's call to the station, when he reported the shooting. We both stipulated to let it in. They're using it to show how calm he sounded, and I'm using it to make sure the jury knows that Tony did in fact report the crime at least five or ten minutes before the cops arrived, giving him plenty of time to get that empty casing out of his gun - if he knew it was there.

Their next witness is the police supervisor who was first on the scene. They make sure that a cop calling in a shooting death is responded to by someone in a supervisory position instead of some rookie beat cop. The cop testifying is no young punk, and having been on the job at least fifteen years, he knows who Tony is, and it looks like he's feeling the pressure of being torn between trying to put a bad guy away and trying to protect a fellow police officer.

When the D.A. is through with him, I only ask a few questions about Tony's cooperation. This cop has made a lot of arrests, and I want him to let the jury know that Tony didn't act like the typical guy who was guilty of something. This is another link in my chain of events that I hope will lead the jury to believe that Tony had no idea that empty shell casing was in his gun when he called in the crime and surrendered his weapon to the police.

A forensics lab tech is next, and after the supervising cop identifies Tony's gun and the five shells removed from it, the tech testifies as to all five of them. He tells the jury that four of them were still unfired and the one empty shell casing was in the cylinder in the exact place it should be if it the gun had just fired the fatal shot.

Responding to a well-prepared set of questions, he also brings in some blow-ups of pictures taken of two fired shell casings, both from Tony's weapon. One of them is the empty one that they found in the cylinder and another is one of the unfired rounds that they subsequently fired in the testing lab. The purpose of this display is to show the marks left on both casings from the firing pin and being slammed back against the breech. The tech shows that the firing pin indentation and breech mark patterns are identical on both bullets. In his expert opinion, they were both fired from the same weapon: Tony's gun.

He does an adequate job of testifying to what the D.A. wants. On cross-examination, I get him to repeat how positive he is that both shells were fired from Tony's weapon and then ask him the one question I want to pin him down with. "Can you testify with any certainty as to when the empty shell casing you found in the defendant's weapon was fired?"

There's no way he can answer that question, because it's impossible to tell the passage of time between firing of the shells without any formation of rust. This is another little link in my perfect frame scenario. When I ask him whether or not he can definitely testify if the empty shell casing he found in Tony's gun had been fired at eight PM on the night of the murder, or at three that afternoon, he answers that he can not.

On re-direct, the D.A. stresses the fact that Tony's fingerprints were found on that empty shell, as well on the other four rounds in the cylinder. That's when she springs the big question about any other fingerprints, and the tech responds that on the empty shell casing alone, there was another set of partial prints and that they appear to be from a child.

That's all the press has to hear. They knew it was coming, and this is the high point of the trial they were waiting for. There is conversation and buzzing throughout the whole large room. The judge bangs his gavel a few times and makes some empty threats about clearing everyone out, before order is finally restored.

On re-cross, I simply wave that testimony aside by getting him to admit that it would have been more surprising not finding a gun owner's prints on the ammunition in his own gun. As to the other set, I'm able to elicit testimony to the effect that just because there were some other person's prints on the casing, there is no way he could tell when they got there or if they were placed there when the shell was put into the gun's cylinder. He finally admits that some of Tony's prints overlapped the child's prints, so it's likely that Tony handled the shell after the child did.

Their next witness is the lab tech who processed all of the prints on the shell casing. He explains how fingerprints removed from items were matched to prints already on file. His display shows both sets of fingerprints and identifies the persons they belong to as the defendant and one Suzi Braunstien. There's a little more whispering, but not enough to disturb the judge. I assume that it was about forty people all saying the same thing under their breath - something to the effect that the kid is related to me.

After a short break so that the jury can stretch their legs, the judge lets us all know that he only expects the D.A. to put on two or three other witnesses and that they will probably rest their case some time shortly after we come back from lunch. In all the felony cases I've ever been involved with, I've never seen one go so fast. It's the perfect case.

It's now time for them to establish Tony's motive, so they bring in two witnesses. First Renaldo, who reluctantly testifies to the fact that Tony and Joe had argued quite a few times and in his opinion, they almost came to blows.

On cross-examination I get Renaldo to admit that he's argued with his girlfriend many times, in as heated a fashion as Tony and Joe did, but he never contemplated killing her. That neutralizes his testimony.

Their last witness is a black activist who claims that there have been more complaints to him about Tony's excessive use of force on black people then on any other policeman in his precinct. I don't have any questions for him, because I think his testimony antagonized the jury more than it established Tony's motive.

They saved their best for the last. The judge looks down at the D.A. and makes way for their final witness. "Do the People intend on calling their last witness now? And if so, is it the one we discussed earlier today in chambers?"

"Yes, Your Honor. With the Court's permission, we would like to call her now."

"Just to cover all the bases Mister Sharp, do you have any objection you'd like to make for the record?"

I stand up to give him my answer. "No Your Honor." This lets the judge, jury, court reporter and the press know that this is okay with me. The judge feels that he should let the jurors in on the cast of characters now so that the record will reflect everyone's informed consent to the witness appearing and the relationships involved.

"Ladies and gentlemen of the jury, the People's last witness will be called to the stand shortly, and I want to state for the record, the unique set of relationships in the courtroom today. This witness was the orphaned stepdaughter of an attorney who died in a plane crash not too long ago. Upon his death he left instructions that his close friend, neighbor and business associate should be appointed as the child's legal guardian. This last wish of his was granted by another branch of this court. The witness being called is a young girl. Normally, we would insist on her having a parent or guardian present, but that's not necessary in this situation, because her legal guardian is already here. He's the defense attorney in this case, Mister Peter Sharp.

"And, for a complete disclosure of all the pertinent facts, you should be aware that Mister Sharp is the former husband of Myra Scot, this prosecutor's boss, the District Attorney of our County, who is also a close friend of the witness, and who I see has just entered the courtroom and is sitting in the back row. Good afternoon, Miss District Attorney." Myra nods back to the judge.

This announcement probably isn't news to anyone but the jurors, but there's still quite a bit of whispering going on in the gallery. The judge knows that this is a singly unique situation, so he gives the whisperers a chance to finish and then gives the D.A. a nod that it's okay to go ahead. Witnesses in criminal cases are not allowed to sit in the courtroom during a trial. This is so that they don't have an opportunity to hear what other witnesses have testified to. Witnesses who have not yet been called are either seated in some nearby waiting room or must wait outside in the hall.

The prosecutor stands up and calls Suzi Braunstien to the stand. At this point, the rear door to the courtroom is held open, and the little brat princess, who had been waiting outside in the hall slowly starts her long walk to the witness stand. When everyone sees that doll-face of hers, a chorus of oohs and aahs can be heard, similar to the sound a movie audience makes when they see some adorable puppies on the screen.

The kid knows what's going on, so she takes her sweet time getting to the swinging gate that leads to the counsel tables area. A bailiff was stationed at the gate, and he opens it for her so that she can easily walk through. At this point, I'm wondering why she didn't tuck a little teddy bear under her arm for a bigger emotional affect.

As she slowly walks through the gate, she does something that completely astounds me while at the same time informs me that she's choreographed her appearance today, down to every movement she makes. She walks over and plants a kiss on my cheek. At the same time she's kissing me, I feel her press a folded sheet of paper into my hand. I can't stop to look at it now. She then takes the witness stand. I don't know if the audience can notice it, but everything from my neck up feels like it's on fire. I hope that Court TV has a color camera working here today, because I'm probably now a glowing red.

This portion of her act draws more oohs and aahs from the crowd. I look back to see if I can catch Myra's eye, and I do. She is looking at me, and from our exchange of knowing glances, I realize we both appreciate the fact that the kid is playing this packed courtroom like a pinball machine. I have no doubt that in less than five minutes, the kid will have every person in this courtroom wrapped around her little finger.

I was wrong. It didn't take five minutes. When she sat down in the witness chair, she looked up at the judge and gave him an innocent smile. He smiled back at her. Mission accomplished, and it took less than a minute. I hope she realizes that as an adult attorney someday, she'll have to change her act.

Every witness who takes the stand in any kind of hearing is usually sworn in by the Court Reporter, at which time they are expected to raise their right hand and swear to God that they will 'tell the truth, the whole truth, and nothing but the truth.' In this particular case, the judge, already having been wrapped around the kid's finger, has decided to take on this task himself.

He looks down at her and starts to explain how important it is to tell the truth, and not to lie when asked a question. Little does he know that the person he's talking down to has an IQ much higher than his own, and thinks he's some kind of ignorant jerk who's wasting her time. She goes along with the act and promises him that she'll be truthful to all of the grown-ups who will be questioning her. He nods at the D.A., letting her know that it's okay for her to start her questioning. She stands up and begins the questioning, following instructions she received from the judge in chambers, she is extremely courteous to the kid. We decided that it would be best to address this witness as 'Suzi.'

"Suzi, I'm the deputy district attorney here today, and I work for your friend Myra. She wants me to ask you a few questions about a bullet. Is that okay with you?"

The kid innocently nods affirmatively. She knows damn well that she's supposed to say 'yes,' because the court reporter needs her words for the record, but she's obviously doing this so that the judge will talk to her. He jumps at the opportunity to let the huge television viewing audience see what a sweetheart he can be with this small frightened child on his witness stand.

"Suzi honey, you're going to have to say yes or no out loud. The court reporter hasn't learned how to take nods for an answer." The court reporter doesn't look too happy about that remark, but takes it down anyway.

Suzi nods, and then lets out an almost imperceptible "yes," at which time the judge shouts at the bailiff to hurry up and turn on the witness microphone. The microphone is turned on and the judge asks her to repeat her answer, which she does. The judge doesn't realize that as of this moment he is no longer in control of the courtroom. It belongs to the kid. She's totally running this show and he's just along for the ride, along with the rest of us.

I'm pretty sure that every eye in the courtroom, including the television camera's lens, is focused entirely on the kid and probably will stay that way every minute that she's on the witness stand. This gives me an opportunity to unfold the sheet of paper she handed me and see what it is. I look to my side and see that Tony is taking everything in, including the paper that the kid passed to me.

Once I discreetly lift it up to the counsel table, I slip it into a stack of papers in front of me and then search for it, just in case anyone's actually watching me, which I doubt. The sheet now looks like something I brought into court with me, like all my other papers. I take a look at it and see that it is a list of questions to ask two witnesses: her and Tony.

The D.A. is now asking Suzi some questions to find out if she knows what a fingerprint is. Little does she know that this witness has a more sophisticated fingerprint analysis capability in her bedroom that the District Attorney's entire scientific investigations department has.

After the D.A. has finished her 'Dick and Jane' explanation of fingerprints, she brings out an evidence exhibit to show the kid. It's the expended shell casing.

Many years ago when I was growing up in Chicago, I liked to play pool and billiards, and the best place to do that was downtown at a place called Bensinger's. They had about five floors of pocket pool, billiards, and snooker tables there, and every hustler in town had his favorite table, where he would make a decent living off of sailors and other tourists who thought they were pretty good players.

One of the most successful hustlers there had what we called a 'drunk act,' during which this old man would practice on a table by himself and miss quite a few shots, while loudly proclaiming he can beat anyone in the place. It worked well for him, because there would always be some young kid like me around who was the best player in his neighborhood poolroom and figured it's about time someone taught that loud old drunk a lesson in how the game should be played.

To make it a little more interesting, the old drunk would suggest that they put a couple of bucks on the game, to which the challenger always agree.

They would start playing and the old man would always lose the first two games. He would then loudly demand a chance to get even by playing for 'double or nothing,' and the challenger would be shamed into giving him the chance. Again, the old man would lose, but by a much closer margin than the first three games. Finally, he would spring the trap and demand one final game to prove that he's the best. After insulting his young challenger repeatedly, by this time the tourist had no sympathy for the old drunk, so he would agree to play the one last game and increase the amount of the bet.

At this time the old drunk would insist that a third party hold the bet money, and each would hand over whatever the stakes had reached to the cashier of the place. Sometimes the bet for that last game would be several hundred dollars. There was also a lot of side betting going on, between the regulars and the tourist's friends.

Amazingly, as the game progressed, the old drunk seemed to suffer less from the influence of alcohol, and actually looked like he was sobering up a bit. The end was actually pre-determined, because the tourist never had a chance. The old drunk would always win by just a point or two, so that the disappointed tourist would blame it on 'luck.' But nevertheless, he lost.

It's been many years since I've seen a good hustler work at Bensinger's, but what the kid is doing to this courtroom reminds me of the old drunk. She has nothing to sober up from, but the routine she's pulling is similar. She started out as an intimidated little waif who couldn't even speak loud enough to be heard without a microphone. I've got a feeling that in a little while when the stakes get raised, her testimonial age will increase to that of an adult.

The D.A. shows the expended shell casing to Suzi and asks her if she recognizes it. Suzi's age goes up a year or two with this answer. "Yes, that's a .50 caliber shell casing, like the kind my friend Tony uses in his gun." This not only shows how smart she is, but also tells the jury that this big muscular cop, who is accused of murder, is friendly with this adorable little witness. It also acts like a non-verbal, favorable, character witness statement.

She is then asked whether or not she put that casing into Tony's gun. "Oh, no, I never load his gun."

The prosecutor is trying to establish that this shell casing was handled by Suzi and then by Tony, and that they were the only ones who had access to it. If Suzi didn't put it into Tony's gun then Tony must have done it himself.

Several years ago, there was a trial in Los Angeles in which a well-known football player named O.J. Simpson was charged with murder. At one point in the trial, one of the prosecutors made what turned out to be a fatal mistake when he asked the defendant to put on a glove that was supposed to have been worn by the murderer. The D.A. wanted to show that it fit the defendant 'like a glove.' For those of us who are courtroom history buffs, we all know how badly that experiment went.

In this case, the prosecutor has just made her fatal mistake, and she's about to pay the price for it. She wants to get the kid to admit that Tony must have put that bullet in his own gun. The D.A. must think that being an average kid, there is a fear that she might be getting blamed for doing something that she didn't do. A normal kid would immediately try to point the finger of suspicion in another direction, and this D.A. hopes that the kid will finger Tony as the one who did the loading. Boy, did she misjudge this witness. The kid was several steps ahead of her before she even walked into the courtroom... and here it comes.

"Suzi, if you didn't put this bullet casing into the defendant's gun, do you think it was put in by someone else?"

Suzi hesitates before answering. I'm sure the little ham is doing it for effect, to bring the courtroom to complete silence. She finally answers quite clearly, and the microphone is not necessary when she gives her answer. "Yes, earlier that day."

In all the years I've been practicing, I've never heard silence like this one. Pens stop writing and people stop fidgeting. There is no coughing. There is no movement. Everyone is frozen in place, listening for the rest of the kid's answer. She looks at the prosecutor and states with certain conviction "Yes, I know who put this shell casing in Tony's gun, but it wasn't Tony."

The silence ends with a bang. There's bedlam in the courtroom, and no matter how much the judge bangs his gavel down, it doesn't stop. The prosecutor is completely flummoxed, and starts to desperately go through the maze of paperwork on the counsel table in front of her. Myra sees the disaster that just happened and comes up to assist her trial deputy, as they re-group to go on with their questioning.

When the noise subsides, Myra stands up and addresses the court. "Your Honor, with the Court's permission, I would like to step in and assist in this matter by continuing to question the witness."

The judge waves his hand to Myra, as if to say 'be my guest.' She thanks him and asks the witness another question.

"Suzi, you've just told us all that you think this shell casing was put into the Defendant's gun earlier in the day. How can you possibly know that?"

I'm sorry to see Myra jump into the hole that the kid dug for her trial deputy. The Law of Holes states that 'when you're in a hole, stop digging.' Not only does Myra completely ignore the rule, she asks for a bigger shovel. The kid waits a few seconds before answering. I can see that once again she's playing the room for effect. She finally gives her answer.

"Because it's not a factory round. It's a re-load, and Tony never uses re-loads anywhere but at the target range. All the other times he keeps the gun loaded with factory rounds."

The audience doesn't know it, but the kid has long ago passed through the little girl part of her act and is now rapidly approaching adult expert witness status. Myra's in a tough spot now, like a person who's hanging on to a mooring rope attached to a blimp. When the blimp gets blown away by the wind, a quick decision must be made to let go of the rope and drop to the ground, because if you don't do it in time, you're lifted up into the air and have to hang on for dear life. Myra's hanging on for dear life now, and the kid knows it. Myra goes ahead.

"Suzi, assuming what you say is true about the Defendant's choice of ammunition, what makes you think that this shell is a re-load instead of a new factory round?"

That's it. The kid has given Myra enough rope. Myra put the noose around her own neck, and the kid is now about to tighten it. She looks up at the judge.

"Mister Judge, I can tell Myra how I know that this shell casing is a re-load, but in order to do it, I'll need the help of my assistant. Can I please call him into the room, so that I can show everyone here how I know that's a re-load?"

That 'Mister Judge' did it. He immediately melts down to a point where she could ask him to let her try on the robe, and he probably would take it off then and there and hand it to her. He looks down at her and gives her the answer she expects.

"Of course, my dear." The judge then looks up and speaks to a bailiff standing near the rear entrance doors. "Bailiff, please go out into the hallway and bring in this witness' assistant."

The bailiff opens the rear doors, but he doesn't have to go out into the hallway to find the kid's assistant, because the assistant walks in all by himself. I'm amazed that she actually did it to us. Here comes the Saint Bernard walking down the aisle, heading for the open gate towards the witness stand. More bedlam in the court, because everyone stands up to look down at the dog and sees that he's been fitted with a special leather harness that has two baggage containers – one on each side, much like the burros you would see carrying things for the gold prospectors in old movies. I now realize what the shoemaker was doing on our boat that day. One baggage container has Tony's re-loading press, and the other holds his powder measurement device.

The dog comes around to the side of the witness stand and stays there, waiting for instructions. It takes another minute or two, but order is finally restored. The judge looks down at the kid. "This is your assistant?" She answers with a 'yes.' The judge asks another question. "He isn't going to testify today, is he?"

This time she gives him the line that she must have been working on for several days. It comes complete with a little smile. "No, silly, he's only a dog."

Ordinarily, anyone who addresses a judge as 'silly' is certainly assured of a reprimand, a fine, or a jail cell. This time it was timed perfectly, and the judge laughs, along with the rest of the courtroom spectators, including the jury. Myra and I both look at each other, realizing that no matter what the verdict is, we've both lost today and the kid has won. Not only has the kid taken over control of the judge, she also owns the bailiffs. She asks one of them to bring over a milk crate for her to stand on, and another bailiff to remove the items from her assistant's harness and put them on the small demonstration table that was brought over for her to work with.

Once the equipment is set up, she stands on the milk crate and starts her demonstration with a lecture.

"Whenever a bullet is fired from a gun, the explosion forces the empty shell casing to change its size. It can get wider, longer, or both. If you want to re-load it to use again, you must put it into a press like this so that you can force it back into the size it originally was, or it won't work in the gun." I see that Tony is looking at her like a proud parent.

As she speaks, she gives the court a demonstration, using an empty shell casing that her assistant brought in. As I look around the courtroom, I see that everyone is nodding, as if they are in total agreement with everything she's saying.

"When you use the press to change the size of the shell, the press makes what are called 'sizing marks' on the outside of the casing. These sizing marks aren't always visible to the naked eye, but you can see them with a microscope. The empty shell that was shown to me before has sizing marks on it, so I know it's a re-load. I also know it's a re-load because a friend of mine let me use his 'bore scope' to look inside the shell, and compare the gunpowder residue with gunpowder residue from a factory round. A microscopic comparison showed that the powder we used for re-loading was a different composition from the factory powder residue. A gas chromatograph confirmed our findings."

All during this testimony, the entire viewing public both inside and outside of the courtroom are no better off than that kid who was being hustled at Bensinger's Poolroom in Chicago. That kid didn't notice the old hustler gradually sobering up, and the audience here doesn't notice this kid witness morphing from cute little waif to brilliant forensic examiner.

When she finishes her lecture, she tells Bernie to go wait in the hall. At least I think that's what she told him, because the command was given in Chinese. The dog promptly obeys and walks back through the gate and through the courtroom exit doors that are being held open for him. It's doubtful that the Chinese command will ever appear on this African-American court reporter's transcript of the trial. It also serves to let the audience know that Suzi is fluently multilingual, which adds to her intelligence and credibility in the minds of the jurors. I see that there is an Asian woman on the jury, and she can't seem to be able to wipe an ear-to-ear smile off of her face.

Myra finally decides to quit while she still may have a chance to salvage her case. I inform the court that as far as the Defense is concerned that the kid may be excused now, but that I may be calling her as a defense witness when I present our case.

In a criminal trial the usual procedure is for the witnesses not be allowed to watch each other's testimony, but in this case I make a strange request of the judge.

"Your Honor, we realize that non-testifying witnesses are usually excluded from the courtroom, but as you know, the Prosecution is always allowed to have a witness at their counsel table if he or she is their investigator. In this case, we do intend to recall this child to the witness stand, but we ask the court's permission to let her remain at our counsel table as our investigator and technical expert."

The judge thinks about it for a moment as he looks down at Suzi. She looks up at him with the same pleading expression that might appear on the face of a cocker spaniel puppy about to be put to sleep at the dog pound. There's no way the judge can refuse that face, and every person in the courtroom but the judge immediately realizes it, so his answer is no surprise to anyone. "Well counselor, this would be the youngest investigator I've ever allowed to remain at the table, but I can't see any harm in it, and it would give me a chance to see her a little more." Boy, she sure has him by the nose ring.

Myra doesn't even waste her time by trying to object. Instead, she stands up and tells the judge that the People rest their case. The judge asks me if we're ready to go ahead with our defense, and I tell him that we only have two witnesses. He signals me to proceed, and I call the Defendant, Tony Edwards to the stand. The kid sits next to me on the telephone directory that one of her bailiffs brought over from the witness stand. She's close enough to tug at my elbow if she thinks I'm making a mistake or forgetting to ask a question.

Tony walks over to the witness stand and gets sworn in by the court reporter. I have the kid's list of questions on the table in front of me. Looking down at them, I start to see which direction she wants me to go. I start with the basics, establishing that he is in fact the owner of the .50 caliber gun in the D.A.'s exhibit, and that he absolutely did not shoot the victim.

Next I have him tell the jury that in his opinion re-loads are not dependable enough in life-and-death situations, so it is against his department's policy to have a weapon loaded with them for any other purpose but target practice.

We go into the details of his ammunition purchasing and show that only one box containing 20 rounds was purchased for normal use, and another five boxes were purchased for practice and re-loading purposes only. Suzi is tugging at my sleeve and pointing to a group of questions on the list. I get the feeling that she's exerting a great deal of control by restraining from jumping up and trying to take over the questioning herself.

After the ammo stuff is covered, we go into a series of questions that explain why he prefers to re-load the shells, and the economics of spending up to three dollars each for new factory round is compared to the costs of powder, bullet head and other incidentals required for re-loading. Tony explains how a pound of gunpowder contains seven thousand grains, and that a re-load can use as few as 25 grains, making the pound good for at least 280 re-loads. A twenty-dollar pound will mean that each re-load costs only seven or eight cents. That amount added to a twenty-cent replacement bullet head keeps the average cost of each re-load down to less than fifty cents, including the primer and other items required. This represents a savings of over 2.50 on each re-loaded shell and can save a serious target shooter up to a thousand dollars a month.

I then ask him to explain why it is not proper to use re-loads for anything but practice. At this point Myra makes a relevancy objection, but I'm able to convince the court that this information is necessary for us to show why a re-load would not be in Tony's gun unless someone else planted it there. Her objection is overruled, so we go on to learn that there have been too many incidents where re-loaded ammunition has mis-fired or jammed a weapon. This is bad enough when it takes place on a practice range, but no experienced peace officer wants to take a chance like that in a life-or-death situation, so when not on the range, only brand new factory rounds are used.

Now that we may have convinced the jury that Tony would never have put a re-load into his revolver for use outside of the practice range, I feel that we may be on the way of creating some reasonable doubt about his guilt. At least I'm finally starting to think he might be innocent.

Knowing how much ammunition Tony usually uses at the practice range, we discuss how he manages the rounds. He explains that he uses a Speed-Loader, into which five bullets are placed. Before going to the range, he will load about twenty of the Speed-Loaders with the re-loaded ammunition he plans to fire that afternoon. Each Speed-Loader is a cylindrical device that lines up with the empty slots in his gun's cylinder. After he finishes firing off the five rounds his gun carries, he swings the cylinder out, dumps the empty rounds into his 'brass basket,' uses the Speed-Loader to insert five re-loaded cartridges into his cylinder at one time, swings his cylinder shut, and tosses the empty Speed-Loader into the brass basket. During this entire period of time, the five factory rounds that were in his weapon when he got to the range are in his trousers pocket, ready to be re-inserted into his cylinder at the end of the day.

This same procedure is repeated each time he goes to the practice range. He brings with him a basket containing twenty Speed-Loaders, each with five cartridges, and goes home with the same basket containing twenty empty Speed-Loaders and one hundred spent shell casings.

I feel a tug at my sleeve and see that the kid is pointing at the next group of questions. By looking ahead earlier, I can tell where she's going, so I decide to continue the rest of my examination not sitting next to her. I'm afraid if I stay seated at the table while she keeps tugging at my arm and pointing to the list of questions, it'll look like she's the ventriloquist, which leaves only one remaining role for me to be playing.

We discuss what clothing Tony usually has on while he's shooting at the practice range and he describes the 'lucky' Rugby shirt he likes to wear. It's the one he wore many years ago during a shooting competition that he won. When I ask him whether or not he wears it to and from the range or changes there, Myra pops up with another relevancy objection. I make an Offer of Proof to the judge. That gives me a little leeway here and means that if I don't show that these questions were actually relevant, the whole line of testimony can be stricken from the record. He accepts my offer and Tony is allowed to continue with his answers. He explains that there is a changing room at the range, so he usually carries the Rugby shirt in the brass basket and puts it on before shooting, removing it at the end of the session.

At this point I start to zero in on the exact end-of-the-day routine. Step by step we re-create Tony's every move, from the time he finishes firing off the last round of the day, to the time he gets into his car to leave the range. His progress is as follows. He finishes shooting the last practice round, empties the cylinder into the brass basket, loads the five factory rounds from his pocket back into the cylinder, and walks to the changing area.

Once inside the changing room, he struggles for as many as fifteen or twenty seconds trying to remove the Rugby shirt, which fits tighter every year due to a loss of elasticity in the shirt and Tony's muscles getting bigger. I stop him right there with some pivotal questions.

"Detective Edwards, while you're struggling to get out of the tight Rugby shirt, where is your gun."

"It's on the bench, right next to my brass basket."

"If your Rugby shirt is a tight enough fit to take fifteen seconds to get it over your head, does that mean for a short period of time the gun is out of your sight?"

He answers this in the affirmative, and I press on.

"Is this changing area private, or are other shooters allowed to use it at the same time that you do?"

He thinks for a few seconds before answering. "Yeah, some other shooters may be in there at the same time. We hang around for a while exchanging war stories. It's mostly a lot of cops that use the range."

"Detective, how long would it take someone to pick up your gun, swing out the cylinder, remove a factory round, insert an empty shell casing, and then put your gun back down in the same place?"

I can see that Tony is visualizing the entire process in his mind, counting off the number of seconds it might take.

"Probably less than ten seconds."

"So in other words, what you're telling us is that while you're struggling to pull a tight garment over your head, your gun is out of your sight for up to twenty seconds, and someone could have performed the acts I questioned you about and still have ten seconds to spare. Is that correct?"

Bingo. I see some light bulbs going off over the heads of a couple of jurors. Turning around to return to my seat, I also see some serious scribbling going on in the gallery.

"Sure, I guess that someone could do that without me noticing it."

At this point I have no further questions to ask him, so I tell the judge I'm through with him for now, and let Myra have a shot at him. Now I'm amazed for the second time this afternoon. Myra passes. The prosecution has no questions for Tony.

This is unheard of. There isn't a prosecutor in the world that doesn't salivate at the chance of having a shot at the defendant in a criminal trial. It's too good an opportunity to pass up. The only reason I can figure out for her passing up a chance like this is that she's starting to get the idea that I might win this case, and she doesn't want to come off too harsh against a police hero who might get acquitted. Smart move on her part. She wants to live to fight again another day.

By the time I get back to my seat, Tony is out of the witness seat and back to his chair next to me at the counsel table. I call my next witness.

"The defense calls its investigator and technical expert, Miss Suzi Braunstien."

She hears her name and jumps right up to her seat in the witness box, barely giving the bailiff a chance to bring the telephone directory over and slide it under her rear end before she plumps down and starts adjusting her microphone.

She gives a subtle smile to her new friend the judge. He returns it in kind, so I know that she's still in control of the courtroom. I check over her list of questions and know what to ask, but I have no idea what the answers will be. This is not a comfortable situation for any lawyer to be in during a trial, but I have to trust her on this one. I start out by showing her the prosecution's exhibit of that empty shell that they removed from Tony's gun.

"Suzi, you've seen this exhibit when you testified earlier today. Do you have any way to tell when it was fired?"

To the amazement of me and everyone else in the courtroom, she answers.

"Yes."

Another round of whispering goes on and this is a four-gavel-bang disturbance. I've already stuck my neck out by starting with this line of questioning, so I might as well go all the way. I ask the next question.

"Would you please tell the court when you think this round was fired, and also explain the facts you base your opinion on?"

Myra is up and out of her chair making an objection on the ground that only an expert can offer an opinion as evidence. I don't have to say a word, because the judge reminds Myra that both sides agreed in advance by stipulation to letting her testify as an expert. Now Myra finally realizes what the kid has done to her. With the objection discussion resolved, Suzi continues with her answer.

"First of all, knowing that the empty shell casing was planted in Detective Tony's gun while he was changing at the range, it must have been at the end of his shooting session, because I saw him return to the Marina before five PM that day. The shell must have been planted between three and four PM that afternoon."

No whispering in the court, but plenty of scribbling and pressing of keys on the reporters' laptops. Suzi hesitates for a second, as if to gather her thoughts, and then continues on with her answer.

"I figured out the same things that Detective Tony testified to. About the only time someone could have changed the load in his cylinder, but wondered about where the empty round came from. Because his gun was taken away from him that same evening, we never bothered to unload the brass basket and do any re-loading, so I dumped out the contents of the basket and counted the spent shells. There were exactly one hundred of them. This means that if one of them was taken out and planted in his cylinder, whoever did it must have taken it out of the brass basket and tossed in another empty one to replace it.

"Knowing that must have been what happened, I thought that out of the hundred empty casings in the basket, one of them came from the person who did the switch, and that person also must have the same kind of gun. I think that whoever did the switch did the killing."

This time there's more than a whispering in the courtroom. It's loud conversation, and it seems like everyone there is talking to the people seated nearby, discussing the validity of what Suzi just testified to. Myra is talking to her trial deputy, and even the judge is having a brief discussion with one of the bailiffs. Everyone knows that the other shoe might drop pretty soon, so without any banging of the gavel, the room slowly comes back to order. When I hear the commotion die down, I look up at the judge, and he signals for me to continue. By this time, Suzi and I are on the same page.

"Suzi, did you inspect all of the empty shell casings that were in the Defendant's brass basket when he returned from the practice range that day?"

"Yes I did. Whenever a bullet is fired in a gun, the same force that pushes the bullet head out of the front of the gun pushes the shell casing back to the rear of the gun at the same time. This causes what we call recoil, but at the same time it leaves distinguishing marks on the rear face of the shell casing. By carefully examining every one of the one hundred empty shells in the brass basket, I was able to separate out the only one that did not have the same firing pin indentation as the other ninety nine shells."

At this time she reaches into her pocket and holds up a small plastic baggie that contains an empty shell casing.

Another outburst takes place in the courtroom. Myra tells one of the bailiffs to go over and take the shell from Suzi. The Bailiff refuses to make a move until the judge tells him to. When the noise subsides, I go on with my questioning.

"Did you have any way to find out which, or whose weapon fired the questioned shell?

"Yes, I did. I had Detective Sid and Detective Frank, two friends of mine, go out to the practice range in plain clothes. They spent several days out there firing, and with a brass basket full of Detective Tony's empty shells. Every time they saw someone with the same kind of big pistol as Detective Tony's, they managed to pick up a spent shell and replace it with one of Detective Tony's old ones. This way, they were able to bring back a bunch of samples to compare with the one I found in the brass basket."

This is the first time I've heard any of the things she's done on this investigation, and I have to admit that she's really done a great job. I don't know what the rest of her answers are going to be, but I can't wait to find out.

"Suzi, were you able to make a match to any of the casings that your detective friends brought back from the firing range?"

"Yes, I was. One of the weapons used at the range gave us an identical ballistics fingerprint match to the other shell."

This is it. The other shoe is ready to drop. I can't believe that this is actually happening, but I think that the kid is getting ready to identify the real killer. There is a flurry of scribbling and laptop usage. Looking back to the rear doors of the courtroom, I see that the bailiffs are having a hard time keeping more members of the press out. They have now allowed sitting room on the floors of the aisles, so another twenty reporters are now crowded in. I might as well go for it now.

"Suzi, after you made the match you told us about, did you have any way to know what gun it came from or who fired it?"

"Yes Peter, because I had the detectives provide me with a license plate to go along with each shell they brought back. I had them run all of the plates through DMV before giving me the shells to compare, so I know what car the shooter drove, but the detectives don't know yet."

This time the courtroom erupts into a cheering session, like one of those television dramas where they finally remove the puppy from the well, and everyone cries and hugs the person they're standing next to. The judge doesn't even try to quiet them down. We all just wait patiently, because we know that everyone realizes the sooner they quiet down, the sooner Suzi will finish her testimony and name the killer. Most embarrassed of all is Myra's trial deputy, who now realizes what a fool she made out of herself when first trying to explain to this innocent little girl what a fingerprint is. With some order restored, I forge ahead.

"Suzi, would you please tell the court who, in your opinion, is the real killer of Joseph Caulfield?"

Suzi doesn't answer. Instead, she climbs up in the witness chair and motions for the judge to come close because she wants to communicate with him privately. Any other witness who tries a stunt like this is immediately dragged out of the courtroom by the bailiffs, but this is no ordinary witness, so the judge leans over to let her whisper in his ear. A dead silence falls over the courtroom, with everyone trying to hear what she's saying. The judge nods an acknowledgement of her little secret and speaks to us. "I'd like both counsel to approach the bench, please."

Myra and I both exchange shrugs with each other and walk into the well towards the bench. When we get there, the judge has a strange request that he whispers to us.

"I know that both of you are sworn officers of the court, so I hope I'll get some cooperation from you. The witness has made a special request that I can't refuse. She tells me that she won't name the shooting suspect in this case unless you both agree to her demand."

Myra and I both look at each other. If it wasn't for the fact that we were in this crowded courtroom with television covering our every move, there's no doubt in my mind at all that we would be in a knocked-down dragged-out argument about whose fault this is. I try to quietly tell her that she should have never subpoenaed the kid, and she blames me for not knowing what the kid was planning on doing here today. This slightly heated discussion is being conducted in hoarse whispers, as we stand in front of the judge. He interrupts us with his own whisper.

"Counsel, please. This is a criminal court, not divorce court. I can see a slight disagreement the two of you are having about child raising. If you would have stayed married, you could have had this discussion outside of the courtroom. However, you're not still married, and this isn't divorce or domestic relations court, so I'm going to have to stop you for a minute to give me a chance to tell you what this child wants."

Myra and I take his advice and cool down for a second, to give the judge a chance to continue.

"Suzi tells me that she'll give you the name of the person who owns the car that the shooter was driving, if the two of you will take her out to dinner tonight at some Mexican restaurant you've all been to before. And, as an extra bonus, if the two of you will try to spend the entire evening together without fighting, she also promises to testify about some additional evidence she has that may even name the shooter for you."

Myra and I both turn to glare at the witness, who is doing her best 'little angel' impression during this whole discussion. We tell the judge that we'll agree to her terms and return to our respective seats at the counsel tables. I continue with my questioning.

"Suzi, just before this last break, I asked if you have an opinion of who the real killer is. Will you please tell us your opinion now if you have one?"

"Yes, I do have one. In addition to the license plates that my friends ran, they also checked gun sales throughout Southern California and background checks made for those purchases. They concentrated only on the same .50 caliber weapon like Detective Tony has. When all the results came back in, there was a match. We saw only one name that appeared as registered owner of a car at the practice range who also had a background check conducted for the purchase of a .50 caliber Smith and Wesson revolver like Detective Tony's."

A slight commotion is taking place, and a few reporters walk out of the courtroom, to be ready to get to their satellite vans in time to be first to broadcast the name of the killer. All of the other reporters in the courtroom are frantically dialing their cell phones, trying to get connected to their network or associate downstairs at the news van. When it gets quiet enough, Suzi continues.

"The name that turned up as a match all over was David Miller, and I believe that he was the one who had the same gun as Tony, was at the practice range that day, made the ammunition switch, called Detective Tony and told him to meet the victim at the soundstage, and then drove over there to kill the

257

victim knowing that Detective Tony would call it in and get arrested."

Did I hear her right? David Miller is the name of the guy who manages the apartment building where April lives. Suzi isn't through yet. She has another announcement to make.

"Mister David Miller is now out in the hallway. He's in handcuffs, waiting to be formally arrested by the District Attorney."

Any semblance of order is now completely out of the question. People are shouting in the courtroom, trying to get their story told by cell phone. At the same time, the doors to the hallway are jammed with people trying to get out there to see the arrestee and get a picture of him on their new picture phones. When it seems like everyone who wants to get out of the courtroom has succeeded, the judge looks down at Myra and asks her only one question. "Will you be making a motion to dismiss?"

Myra looks up at him and nods assent. The judge looks at Tony and the jury. Detective, you're free to go now. All charges against you have been dismissed. Ladies and gentlemen of the jury, I thank you for your participation in this trial and want you to know that you are also dismissed and free to go home.

It's only now that I realize the seats in the front row of the courtroom are empty. Snell and his men have already escorted the piracy gang out of the courtroom, and I didn't get a chance to say goodbye to Evelyn. Well, that's life. During all the commotion, Suzi slipped out of the witness chair and is now out in the hallway making her press statement, which I'm sure she's rehearsed many times over the past week. I'll have to catch it on the news later tonight.

Looking around, I also see that Tony is gone too. That's strange, because I usually get a thank you after I manage to keep someone's rear end off of death row. After a few minutes, Myra and I realize that we're the only ones left standing. The courtroom is almost empty and all the action is now out in the hall. The judge has left the bench, so we might as well make plans for dinner now. It's decided that Myra will ride in the car with me, so I use my cell phone to call Jack B. and tell him to bring the Hummer around. One of Tony's detectives gives us the message that Suzi will meet us at the restaurant. She and her assistant are riding there in a caravan of police cars.

I still can't figure out how this David Miller fits into the puzzle, so when going out into the hallway I try to get a look at him. There's some slight resemblance to the pony-tailed hippie I met at April's apartment building, but the David Miller they've now got handcuffed here has short curly blonde hair and he's clean-shaven. I'll have Myra ask the kid how she made this connection. I think he was sitting in the back of the courtroom on the first day of trial too, but at that time I must have thought he was just a trial-watcher who got lucky and grabbed an empty seat. If he's really the shooter, then he probably got spooked when Suzi said she'd give him up. He obviously snuck out with the bunch of reporters who were leaving the courtroom to file their stories.

As we leave the courthouse and walk out to the sidewalk where Jack and the Hummer are waiting for us, we see the news crews' camera lights in the parking lot. They're all interviewing the new star, who is precariously standing atop two milk crates. I hope that the New York morning shows are ready to fork over extra first class tickets for her assistant and legal guardian too, because that's the only way I'll agree to let her appear.

15

The victory party at the restaurant is pretty upbeat. When we enter Mi Ranchito we're informed that everything has already been paid for. The entire evening is on Tony, who gave them his credit card number. I look around, but don't see him.

We now hear the sirens of Suzi's escort vehicles. When two of Tony's close cop friends come in, I inquire about Tony, and they tell me that he wasn't feeling too good, so he went home to rest. I don't blame him. We all went through quite a bit with this case, but he's the only one who was in danger of going behind bars. Stress can do a lot of damage - even to a man of steel like Tony.

While we're eating, the restaurant owner tunes the numerous hanging television sets to an English-speaking channel, so we can all watch the local early evening news. The blow-dried newscaster tells us about the motion picture piracy ring bust, and the screen shows Snell being interviewed outside his office. The FBI doesn't like to be seen on TV near a State courthouse, because that level of government is obviously beneath them. Instead, we see him outside the West Los Angeles Federal Building, and he's managed to be interviewed in such a way that the camera can also see the building's identification and flag waving in the background. All he needs now is brass band quietly playing some patriotic John Phillips Sousa march in the background. *Stars and Stripes Forever* would probably suffice.

He owes me big time for this case, and true to his word, his little speech doesn't mention any baloney about how the FBI conducted a lengthy investigation to track down the culprits. Naturally he takes all the credit for the arrest, but he also says that the received some helpful and important information from a private citizen, and the tip was instrumental in leading to the arrest and what will certainly result in conviction of the persons in custody. I never asked him to say anything like that, so I guess he's getting a little soft as he ages and starting to show a little appreciation for us civvies.

The part of the show that we're all most interested in watching comes on screen and the newscaster is seen outside by a news van in the courthouse parking lot. He can't stop gushing on and on about how this brilliant little girl helped crack the case and lead to the detective being cleared of all misdoings. The camera follows her to where two uniformed cops lift Suzi up and stand her on the milk cartons. She's now almost eye-level with the reporters and the cameras, and the interview starts. I see something new added to her wardrobe: she's wearing a baseball cap with some inscription on the front of it, and it looks like it starts out with 'www.' If I'm not mistaken that's her Internet website address, and during the interview she mentions how her forensics laboratory is equipped.

When the reporters ask her how she got all that equipment, she tells him that her legal guardian bought if for his office to use, and she learned how to run the programs, providing help to law enforcement agencies in the area. She did it again. Not only did she just advertise our law firm and its scientific capabilities, but she also managed to prove to me that the equipment was worth the money and that it is now a law firm expense, not to be deducted from her end of the profits.

The really interesting part comes when she gets asked how she felt 'beating' her good friend Myra, to which her practiced reply was beautifully constructed and performed. "I didn't beat her. There was only one loser today, and that was the man they arrested for doing the crime. Everyone else won, because the truth came out, and that's what the District Attorney's office wanted from the beginning. There's no way that Attorney Myra would want to prosecute and send an innocent person to jail, so she won along with the rest of us."

"Well Suzi, you must think a lot of our District Attorney... and also of your legal guardian, Attorney Peter Sharp."

"Oh yes, I do. And when I graduate Harvard Law School and start my own law firm, I intend to hire both of them.

At this point the news turns to more serious stuff, and both Myra and I shoot glances over to our future employer, who is surrounded by so many cops that she doesn't notice our looking at her.

I tell Myra to be careful. "You know something Myra? She means it. I hope I'm retired from practicing law twenty years from now, because that kid over there is what the future will be like. Would you really like to go up against her head-to-head in a trial? I know I wouldn't, and I pity anyone who does."

One of the cops comes over and hands me a note, telling me that it's from the little hero. Unfolding the napkin it's written on, I see five words scribbled. 'I'm tired. Let's go home.'

Myra assures me that the cops will drive her home, so I signal Jack that we'll be leaving and he goes out to get the Hummer. It's a good thing he's our designated driver, because he gave up his heavy drinking many years ago and is now completely clean and sober.

When we get back to the Marina I head right for our boat without stopping to check in on Tony. The lights are all out on his boat, so he must be sleeping already.

It probably will take another few days for me to find out the real story of how this case was solved. I still think there are plenty of things I don't know about.

EPILOGUE

The following morning after our trial ended, everyone noticed that Tony's boat was gone from its slip, but no one knew where it went. Two months later, the kid leaves a box on my desk. She says she found it sitting on the outer deck of our boat, probably left by some cop friend of Tony's. Inside the box are two packages - one large and one small. The large one has my name on it, and the small one has Suzi's.

The outside of the package contains instructions that it is to be given to us two months after the trial ends. Opening up my package first, I find a beautiful rosewood case with an engraved plate attached. It has three initials in it: 'A.C.E.,' which I'm sure stand for Anthony C. Edwards. Inside the case is Tony's .50 caliber Smith & Wesson revolver with a post-it note that says 'you feel lucky Mr. Lawyer?'

I shake the dog biscuit box and give our magically appearing messenger the small package to deliver. After finishing his biscuit, he grabs the package in his mouth and disappears into the guest stateroom below.

A little while later I see the kid wearing a new necklace around her neck that consists of a gold chain from which is hung a leather holder with Tony's police detective badge attached to it. I feel that a warning is in order. "Suzi, I just want you to know that if you want to wear that badge around the boat it's okay, but please don't wear it anywhere else, because that would be against the law."

Oh boy, that does it. Not only is she getting ready to speak to me, but I think I'm in for a lecture.

"Peter, I'm well aware of section 538d of the Penal Code, and it specifically states that in order for the crime to be complete, a person who is not a peace officer, but who is wearing the badge of a peace officer must have the specific intent to fraudulently induce the belief that he or she is a peace officer. Now I ask you, is there any condition under which you could be induced to believe that I am a peace officer if you see me wearing this badge?"

I guess the conversation is over, because she has completed rolling her eyes and is now walking away, disgusted at my feeble attempt to play lawyer. Some day she's going to be grown up, and I pity any guy who gets involved with her... inside or outside of a courtroom.

Gary Fitzpatrick, one of Tony's closest friends and former partner on the police force stops by to say hello and fills me in some facts about Tony. Gary tells me that just before the trial started, Tony put in his retirement papers, and requested that they become effective one day after the trial ended. The department was directed to deposit all of his pension benefits directly into a special account that was set up to provide for the college education of his two young sons.

Gary also tells me that Tony was ill, due to his serving four years in the Navy, working in ships' boiler room. Twenty years ago, before most of the ships were nuclear powered, the boilers were insulated with asbestos and breathing in that dust took its toll on Tony. About a month before the trial he was diagnosed with a lung disease, and the prognosis wasn't too good. He told Gary that after the trial, which he felt confident would go his way, he planned on packing a normal life's supply of pain medication, obtained from a friendly drug dealer, and sailing off into the sunset.

I thought his weight loss was due to the stress of being charged with Joe's murder, but now I learn that it was because of his illness.

There were some other interesting news items recently, including the report that some psychiatrist committed suicide by jumping out of an office building somewhere in Hollywood. His name wasn't released to the public, but I think I know who it was.

Snell had another mini press conference to announce the arrest of a wealthy husband and wife who were operating a white supremist paramilitary training camp on the outskirts of Los Angeles County. They were distributing racist literature, and training groups of people in how to use illegal machine guns. That bothered the government, so Snell was brought in. Quite a bit of helpful information about their group was provided by a former member who is now in custody on a non-related charge. So much for honor between racists.

When they reveal the names of the husband and wife, it suddenly dawns on me that the snitch who turned them in may have been in custody on a charge that actually was related to the couple. Their names are Chad and Ruth Sinclair, and if they are the ones who own the apartment building that April lives in, David Miller must be the former member mentioned.

It's all slowly starting to come together in my mind. The Sinclairs and David Miller all belonged to a white supremist group. This means that when their tenant April started bringing her black boyfriend Joe Caulfield home with her, Miller and the Sinclairs must have gone postal.

Being heavily involved in weapons, it was reasonable to expect them to go to target ranges often, and learning that one of the shooters out there was also working on the black boyfriend's motion picture gave them too great an opportunity to pass up, especially after seeing Joe Caulfield one day when he went shooting with Tony. Miller probably cased the soundstage and planned the whole murder and frame-up, maximizing his access to Tony's gun during those few seconds when it was out of Tony's sight while the tight rugby shirt was being removed.

With the Sinclairs and Miller all in custody, the real estate trust was in financial trouble, so it filed for bankruptcy. From what April tells me, the referee in bankruptcy appointed a receiver to supervise the apartment buildings, and he hired April to be the manager of the building she lives in.

She also has lost more than fifty pounds already, and Hershel's weight loss business is doing as well as his dealership. This must be great for Hershel's supplier, who is my friend Stuart, now semi-retired in his late uncle's condo in Thailand, on the island of Koh Sumai.

April is now engaged to a black gentlemen she met at Hershel's dealership, where he's the assistant general manger of new car sales. When their wedding announcement is made public, I hope she isn't disappointed by not getting a congratulatory card from the Sinclairs.

After Myra got a guilty verdict in Miller's murder trial, we got together for dinner again, and she told me the information she wormed out of the kid, as to how the case was really solved. Hearing how it was done is a lot like watching some fabulous magician create the most fantastic illusion you've ever seen and then discovering how easy the trick was to perform. That's why I never watch those TV shows featuring masked magicians who give away all the secrets of their trade.

When Myra asked Suzi when she dis-covered that the empty casing in Tony's cylinder was a re-load, Suzi's answer was cryptic, so Myra recreated her conversation with the kid for me:

"Suzi, how long did it take you to determine that the shell casing we took out of Tony's gun was a re-load that was fired earlier that day?"

"Less than a second."

"What? Are you serious? How could you have known so quickly? Did you have some information that we didn't have?"

"Someone told me."

"Suzi, you have to tell me who told you that, because whoever it was may have been connected to the murder in some way. There's no other way that a person could have had that information unless they were involved. Now please tell me, who told you?"

"You did."

"What do you mean I told you? I didn't know that until you revealed it in court that day. I never told you that, Suzi."

"Yes you did. Not directly, but in an interview. As soon as you said that they found another set of prints and that they appeared to be those of a child, I knew right then and there that it was a re-load. It didn't even take a full second for me to be sure of it."

"Okay, so you got some information from my press conference, but I never said any of the other things you were so sure of, so how did you form your conclusion?"

Myra explains at this point that the kid just sighed, as if exhausted by the tedious job of explaining things to adults who don't have the brains to figure things out by themselves.

"Well, first of all, Detective Tony never let me touch any live ammunition. He taught me how to re-load his shells, but once they were pressed, re-sized, re-capped, and re-loaded with the 27 grains of powder he used for practice, he took over and crimped the new bullet head onto the shell. That was the only condition he insisted on. I could learn to use the equipment and help him re-load, but I was never to touch a live round.

"Therefore, when you announced that my fingerprints were on the empty shell you found in his cylinder, I immediately knew that it wasn't a factory round, because I was never allowed to touch those."

"Suzi, if you knew this from the beginning, why didn't you tell us?"

"I was going to, but then you subpoenaed me, and I thought it would be better if I told it in court, because I'm trying to get a little more trial experience."

"Yes, but what about Tony? He was charged with murder. If you would have broken the case sooner, he wouldn't have had to suffer that long and go through the trial."

"Oh, I told Detective Tony. We had a good laugh about it, and he said it was okay for me to save it for the trial, because he knew he was going to win and he wanted to see the look on your face and put on a show for all of his friends.

"Besides, at that time I didn't know who the real killer was. I'm very young, you know, and can't just solve every crime immediately... sometimes it takes a few days."

Hearing all this from Myra is a real shocker. I still can't believe how easy it was for the kid to put things together. Myra continues with her story about their conversation.

"Suzi, from what Peter tells me, when they first met, Miller's appearance was completely different than it was when he was arrested. How did you recognize him?"

"Peter gave me his business card one day after going to the apartment building he managed. We were working on a matter for one of the female tenants there. We also sent the card to Victor's lab for fingerprint comparison with the envelope slipped under her door. I believe Peter offered that case to you, but you turned it down.

"Anyway since we already had his name and fingerprints on file, I decided to follow our new forensics lab protocol by entering his driver's license picture into our new facial recognition software program. The way he looked on his driver's license was the same way he looked in court. It was the way that Peter saw him that was the alteration in his appearance. He must have disguised himself when he suspected that his tenant might have someone snooping around the building.

"It was easy to spot him in court, and I had his photo distributed to our team, so there was no way he was going to get away."

"That was nice work, Suzi, but you know, you could have been in a lot of trouble if you accused him of murder and he didn't do it."

"No problem. When we saw him in court on the first day of trial, we figured he'd be back for the second day too, so one of our team got a warrant to search his car and his residence. Because of the metal detectors, we knew he couldn't wear the gun to court, so we figured he'd either leave it at home or in his car, while he was in court.

"About five minutes after he came into court for the afternoon session, the guys found it in his car trunk. At that time I was unavailable to them, because I was a witness who was going to be called back by Peter. While I was sitting in the witness box, one of our guys outside in the hallway had Miller's gun in a plastic evidence bag, and he waved it in front of the little window in the rear door to the courtroom.

"This was our little signal to let me know that not only did they have the gun, but they also conducted a rush-job of test-firing it to get a comparison with that mystery shell that was included in Tony's brass basket. We had the whole case nailed down for you before I mentioned his name in court that afternoon.

"Once he knew how dead-bang we had him nailed to the wall for the murder, it was easy for Snell to get that info out of him on Sinclair's paramilitary group, and the banned machine guns they were using."

"Wow. That was some piece of work. But why were you so interested in helping the FBI? Special Agent Snell never did anything for you, did he?"

"Sure he did. He helped me put together a package that qualifies the four of us for all the reward money that the major motion picture studios will be sending for our information, which Snell mentioned in his press conference as helping to lead to the arrest and conviction of the piracy gang."

"You just said that there are four of you. Who are the four that are sharing the reward money?"

"Me, Peter, and Tony's two young sons. And Myra... I really meant what I said. There'll always be a place for you in my law firm."

Tony's case is now behind us but he'll never be completely forgotten, especially by all the cops here in the Chinese restaurant, where I'm now having lunch and watching them all file in for their once-a-month inter-agency meeting.

Once everyone is seated and enjoying their meals, a hush falls over the room. I look up and see that all eyes in the place are looking to the rear of the restaurant, where two criminal violations are taking place simultaneously, both being perpetrated by the same person... Suzi!

First, she's brought that huge beast of a dog into the restaurant with her as she comes in through the private rear entrance. They both strut through the entire length of the restaurant towards the front door, where there is a table waiting for her, complete with telephone book for her to sit on. I don't know exactly which particular section of the Health and Safety Code she's currently in violation of, but I do believe that other than when assisting the blind, animals are not supposed to be brought into restaurants.

The other remarkable violation is the fact that she's parading herself past table after table of uniformed cops while prominently displaying that detective badge of Tony's around her neck. After the little parade is over, she parks herself at her table near the front door and some small servings of food are immediately brought over to her by the Asian Boys.

I'm sure there isn't one cop in the place who didn't know and respect Tony and I'm also positive that they all know it's his badge she's wearing. I feel in my bones that any minute now she's going to get arrested. They're going to take her and the dog away and I'm going to have to spend the rest of the day getting them both released. I warned her about wearing that badge. She should have listened to me.

I finish my meal. The cops all finish their meals. The kid finishes her meal. Every cop in the place gets up to leave. On the way out of the restaurant, each one of them passes by her table and pats her on the head. There is no arrest. There is silence. One of the cops seems to be wiping something out of his eye. Almost every one of them drops a little piece of food for the dog.

Editor's notes:

All twelve of the Peter Sharp Legal Mysteries can now be ordered from Amazon.com through the publisher's website, where more details are shown. Please visit **www.legalmystery.com**

Also, with the age of digital publishing upon us, it's never too late to make corrections – so if you happen across what appears like a blatant typographical error in this book, please don't hesitate to point it out to the author. He was the last person to sign off on the text, so we have no problem passing the blame onto him. He can be contacted at: gene_grossman@yahoo.com